Rip It Up

Original Japanese edition published by

Bungeishunju Ltd., Japan in 2000

Published by Inpatient Press, 2021

Mercurial Editions, No. 1

Rip It Up

Kou Machida

Translated by Daniel Joseph

Mercurial Editions

FROM THE TRANSLATOR

Nothing is untranslatable, or everything is, or something.

Translators, academics, pundits, and critics will spend the rest of human history (such as it is) debating this question, so for now suffice it to say: the miracle of translation is that it's impossible, but we do it anyway. Kou Machida's books are notoriously difficult to translate, sure. Some of that comes from his lack of concession to literary norms, and some from the breadth of allusion and experience he brings to the table, but here we all are.

Born in the Osaka area in 1962, Machida was exploring the outer reaches of language and art while he was still in his teens as the singer for the seminal punk band INU, writing lyrics with an avant-garde poetic bent that placed them well beyond the bounds of what one generally expects from the genre. In addition to making music, he collaborated with, and appeared in movies by, maverick filmmakers like Sōgo Ishii (*Burst City*) and Masashi Yamamoto (*Robinson's Garden*), then began publishing poetry in the early 1990s and made his prose debut in 1996. It was *Rip It Up* (Jp. Kiregire), however, that brought him widespread acclaim and established him as the enfant terrible of the Japanese literary world when it won the prestigious Akutagawa Prize in 2000. I say "widespread," but Machida's work can be baffling even to native speakers, and he himself told me that "no one" reads him in Japan. This isn't entirely true, of course, since many of the leading lights of contemporary Japanese fiction are die-hard fans: Yoko Tawada, Hiroko Oyamada, Mieko Kawakami, the list goes on.

It is true, however, that his prose isn't for everybody. Structurally far out, uncompromising in its lack of respect for grammar and punctuation...and Machida isn't afraid to bring us inside the minds of truly unpleasant people like the toxic shit heel at the center of *Rip It Up*. There's also a head-spinning density of allusion—from pop music to Camus to Buddhist sutras in the course of just a few pages. Or take the karaoke song near the beginning of the novel, a dense mash-up of lyrics from popular ballads, wartime advertisements, ancient poetry, and famous shogi sayings (?!), the general feel of which, at least, I hope I've been able to convey. Having spent my adult life ping-ponging between singing in punk bands and studying medieval Japanese literature, I like to think I'm as prepared as one could hope to be before entering the labyrinthine library of Machida's prose. Whether or not I've managed to "translate" anything will be yours to judge.

There are some notes at the end of the book on people, places, and cultural concepts that may be unfamiliar, and the only other piece of business to mention is name order. On the cover and here in the translator's note, I've switched people's names from the Japanese order (surname first) to the "English order" (surname last). In the text itself, however, I've maintained the former. This is largely a matter of personal preference, but it's also true that rhythm and prosody are of utmost importance in Machida's work (he's said in interviews that he prizes them over "meaning," whatever that is), and I felt most able to channel the flow of this book by leaving the Japanese name order intact. Hope that doesn't bother you.

- Daniel Joseph

Rip It Up

Innumerable deities dance, Daikokutens and Kisshōtennyos. Water geysers from the windows of buildings on either side of the boulevard as the cheers from the crowd lining the street clump together, howling a single meandering path into the sky. Possessed by a ghost of wild starvation, blossoms like the driven snow. Ribbons in the wind. Which reminds me, when I was taking a taxi from the ANA Hotel towards Shin·Ichi no Hashi, out the lefthand window I saw a gigantic woman's face on the first floor of one of the buildings, staring me dead in the eye with this heinous expression, and, well, I knew right away that it was something unearthly, but with no sleep and no food I'd already been feeling like my own face had been ballooning into one like hers, the whole thing makes me sick. People leaping enthusiastically off a department store roof like celebratory popcorn. My giganticized face dominates the sky, as the next to come plummeting down is my wife. No will of her own, she just yells Geronimo! or something like everybody else. White blouse, legs sheathed in black socks poking obscenely from the airy billows of her red pleated skirt. At first she seemed to be getting into the spirit of the thing with that Geronimo! but sure enough she got cold feet, she turned pale and got goosebumps on her upper arms, but then down she went anyway. Splat. People keep coming down one after another with no sign of stopping, though, so the crowd doesn't seem particularly surprised. But when we've all got half a mind to race in the front door of that red-and-white-striped building, dash up to the roof, and keep the party going by jumping off as well, why *would* they be? It just gets 'em fired up. What a dummy my old lady is, if you're gonna jump off a building, you've gotta wait till the crowd's paying attention, till they're gonna applaud, but she jumped at the exact moment an electric parade float heralded by neon fairies rolled into view around the corner of Mitsukoshi, so not a soul witnessed her swan dive. What a lonely way to go. What a dumbass. Of all the people in the world, why the hell did I marry such a moron, such a dumbass? Pitiful. Disgraceful. I thought, watching my wife eat yakisoba in front of the decorative alcove in the sitting room, a painting of a carp climbing a waterfall hanging on the wall behind a celadon pot thrust full of dead leaves.

My god it's disturbing. When did she become such an eyesore? My wife—eating yakisoba in a chemise, sitting with her legs tucked underneath her and her head so far forward that it's almost like she's kowtowing to her food, looking somehow like an animal as she holds back her drooping hair with her left hand and wrinkles her nose, bringing her face right down to the plate—and the yakisoba itself, I wouldn't eat that grotesque, garish heap of noodles for all the money in the world.

The dim interior of the house is in complete and total disarray. Six-mat room four-and-a-half-mat room three-mat room and a bathroom kitchen tiny yard. Japanese architecture on the skids, from the sliding doors to the latticed shutters to the bamboo fence to the tiled floor in the entryway and the single step up into the house. Plants and animals carved into the wooden transoms. The outside of the house is just as dismal. The paint must've been a bright white at some point, but now it's brown like burnt tea. The veranda's lost its color as well, and the birdbath has that foolish red rope tied around it. A palm tree sticks out among the weeds like a sore thumb. In these dim, dismal surroundings crouches the monstrous form of a woman in a chemise, devouring yakisoba like some wild animal. Where do you think we are, the panty bar? Speaking of, maybe I'll go see what's shaking at the panty bar.

Which had been gloomy that time. I'd been dead drunk from the start. The dead drunk part was Kitada's fault, or maybe that Abe guy's. A place like an automobile factory, all concrete, a burgundy Mercedes and some oil drums, a yellow and black rope forming a dividing line, but despite the clear NO TRESPASSING vibes, Kitada and his friend Abe (who I didn't really know) started fucking around like pro wrestlers over there, while a little ways away my silent thoughts were blowin' in the wind. Five minutes or so. Those two clowns were sporadically visible until finally they weren't, and that's when Abe screamed. I went to see what'd happened and found a deep, rectangular hole in the concrete. Kitada was down there, lying between two iron rails or something that were laid across the bottom. I chewed Abe out, but he was too shaken up to be of any use, and finally I managed to help Kitada out of the pit. Can you walk? but he said he was too dizzy. That turned into Then let's find a cab, and I dragged the wobbling Kitada to a gently curving four lane road where we waited for a taxi to come from our right, but I guess it wasn't good timing, or maybe it was that I was standing in the middle with Kitada on my left and Abe on my right, which meant that Abe would be the first one to see a cab if it came, but this Abe guy was a real blockhead. He didn't react at all when the first taxi appeared. Nothing but a faint *oh* once it was already past. Which is why you don't go doing stupid shit like playing pro wrestlers, alright? Because now Kitada had gone all limp and it was up to me, I had to hail the cab. I guess it wasn't meant to be, though, because taxis were slamming by in record numbers but they were all occupied, not a single empty cab went by, and as we waited, Kitada started trembling like Jell-O, but right when I was asking him Are you OK? was the one and only time an empty cab drove by, at which point I got really pissed. Since Abe was standing furthest to the right you'd expect him to pay attention to the passing taxis, to raise his hand when an empty one appeared and then everything would be hunky dory. But while I was asking Kitada if he was OK, Abe was peering down at his face right along with me, so he completely missed the taxi. Concentrate on the cabs! I shouted at him, but I had a feeling I was never going to be able to rely on Abe to take care of it, so I took it upon myself to stare steadily in the direction the taxis were coming from, but it wasn't my day, because every time it's me, I start keeping a lookout exactly when not only do no empty taxis come but no taxis come at all, the only things going by are massive luxury automobiles and red sports cars that look like they've been molded out of clay, showering us with dust and blaring horns and looks that say *get the fuck out of the way*, because sure, maybe we were sticking out into the roadway a little in an excess of enthusiasm to get a goddamn cab already, and every time this happened I took it out on Abe. If you'd been on the ball we would've been gone ages ago. Don't you feel an ounce of shame just watching a cab go by with the words FOR HIRE in pimply red LED letters on the little readout inside the windshield? Or whatthefuckever, but it didn't do any good, so I fixed my stare, *this time for sure*, and lo and behold, from out of the deepening gloom on the roadway the words FOR HIRE came into view, but the funny thing was that when I thrust out my hand, do or die time, what finally came to a stop in front of us was—what the hell do you call one of those—a taxi van or something, anyway it was a massive taxi that could probably fit eight people, and now I was reluctant to get in. Because Kitada's gone limp, and Abe's clearly worthless, which means that it's me, I'll get stuck with the fare. I know it's not the end of the world, but with this massive taxi the fare will probably be commensurately more massive than it would with a normal taxi. Do I really have to take that on? It's not like I was the one who threw Kitada into a pit. There's this character in the Balzac novel *La Rabouilleuse* called Hochon, who's so stingy that he despises having guests. I understood where Hochon was coming from. Anyway, I told the taxi Thanks but no thanks and sent it on its way. I felt a little guilty, though, so I said to Kitada, You're good, right? That one seemed a little too pricey. And he nodded *yeah, totally*, so I said, It'll be fine, this spot is always crawling with empty cabs, and just as I was saying this, another unoccupied cab sped right by us. What the fuck is Abe doing? I thought, and sure enough, he was nodding along to me and Kitada's conversation. I thought I told you to keep an eye on the taxis, I said, getting more and more pissed off by the second, after which no more empty cabs came and finally I'd had it up to here, I started to feel humiliated, like the taxis were making a fool out of me, so I said Fuck this, you're on your own and went home by myself, and the next day I got a phone call telling me that Kitada had died, so then came the wake and the funeral. Amid the smell of incense and the sound of chanting, every single person, and let's get real it was Abe who threw Kitada into the pit, not me, had this look like I was the one who'd killed him, and everyone was saying, He took off, He just left him there. Talk to Abe, not me, I thought, but he must've been cowering someplace because he was nowhere to be found. Kitada's family was in the grocery business so the place was full of vendors, and those people were all staring me down too. I felt awkward, obviously, so I was guzzling down booze, which made the vendors' faces start flashing blue and red, and behind them Kitada's grandma's and sister's feline faces kept fluttering into view, looking in my direction, their long bright-red tongues flicking out to lick their noses, and as I was watching this display a voice suddenly murmured in my ear, "I guess I shouldn't have let him go to Hokudai after all." It startled me and when I turned around, Kitada's mother was standing there hoisting a bowl piled high with stewed vegetables and looking despondent. Sorry? Hokudai? Kitada went to university in Hokkaidō? But she didn't answer, she just thrust the bowl into my hands and said It's for him. I couldn't stand to be there another minute so I left Kitada's place and went to hold my own solitary memorial service at this panty bar in the old town. Which is where I met my wife.

Plastic flowers and world flags snaked across the ceiling. Every conceivable surface was hung with sparkling pink gauze, the diffuse light hovering in the air. Two little people gotten up to look like Fukusuke dolls tottered over and said something to me but the Bach cantata was so loud that I couldn't make out a word. I gave them my overcoat anyway and followed them to a seat between a woman in white underwear with the head of a horse and a woman in black underwear with the head of an ox, and in front of me three women looking like who knows, some kind of demons, they were in their underwear too, I was surrounded, all of them were whooping and hollering but the cantata was so thunderous that I couldn't catch any of it, and when I yelled, "What the hell is all this?" in the ear of the ox sitting beside me, the ox yelled back in a hoarse voice, "Setsubun monster party," then hopped onto my knee with a bizarrely ululating *EYYYY* and pressed her breast against my nose. While this was going on le champagne arrived, I was fitted out with rubber boobs and a blond wig to match, Cheers, cheers! Cheers! three times and then that strange caterwaul again: *eyyyy*. As if the gauzy cloth hanging everywhere wasn't enough, the only illumination was coming from something that looked like bubbles in green water projected on the walls like we were at a Pink Floyd concert, passing through insubstantial curtains of purple then red, the light tinging the faces of the ox and the horse and the demons, licentious, my face probably looks like that too I thought as I extricated myself from the ox-headed one's breasts to guzzle down more champagne, and suddenly the contents of my head were swelling fit to burst and I wanted to scream away the constricting feeling in my chest, so in wild desperation I cried out like Ox-Head had done, *eyyyy*, *eyyyy*, *eyyyy*, three times, which drove the demons wild with ecstasy, the one that seemed the most demure of the bunch standing up and dancing away to disappear amid the gauze. All of a sudden the cantata broke off, replaced in less than an instant by a melody that existed somewhere in the no man's land between despondency and cheer, the sound of *I'm going to kill myself tomorrow, but I'm gonna make a hell of a lot of noise before I do* blasting out of the speakers at such a ludicrous volume that I could hear the tweeters begin to sizzle. The surging waves of a stormy sea, the surging floats and shouldered reliquaries of a divine parade, numberless as clouds, the throngs beating drums and clanging cymbals as they dance in magnificent unison, a display of fireworks lighting up the sky, and Misora Hibari reigning in state over the cyclorama like a princess of heaven—that kind of melody, that kind of beat. Before I even had a chance to wonder what the hell it was, Horse-Head handed me the mic and the Fukusukes wheeled a massive television on a stand out of the gauzy depths. I stood up, singing at a throat-shredding volume despite having to rely entirely on the words unfurling across the bottom of a screen on which half-naked women in some foreign hut writhed, gnawing at grains of uncooked rice.

It's not unusual to hi-de hi-de hi-de-hi
You're as chaste as ice
And baby we were born to nun
Rollin', rollin', rollin' on Moon River
Any way the lunch grows doesn't really matter

As I sang, my previous misery melted away and I was filled with something approaching bliss, the underwear deities demons Fukusukes raising a cry of joy, stamping their feet, clapping their hands, Viva la monster party! Viva Hawai'i! and I began to sing even louder than before.

Down in the horse corral, gnawing on rice
Hail Hibari, blithe spirit!
Have you anything to say to me?
Do with less – so they'll *have enough!*
Any way the boat rows doesn't really matter

Chicago, Chicago, it's a helluva
Paradise for the losers, power to the people

Give it up, music, tonight only, there is no remorse
Like the remorse of the philosopher's stone
I offer up my life, Okehazamackhackhackhack-hack I'd pushed my throat past the limit and my voice was starting to give out, but I powered through this violent fit of coughing to nail the end of the song and an electrifying euphoria coursed through me, I was elated, when from out of the gauzy recesses to my right something like a slimy soccer ball flew out and slammed into my belly, shouting in a thick Osaka accent, "What the fuck! You fucker, you fucker, who the fuck d'you think you are, fucker!" I was too stunned to speak, whereupon three men in suits burst out of the gauzy depths, a young one a middle-aged one and an older one, grabbing hold of it and saying Sir. Sir. The party's back there, Sir, come on back, and as they started dragging the clammy sphere away it transformed into an old geezer in tortoiseshell glasses, his egg-bald head glistening with sweat. Let's go, Sir. C'mon. But Sweaty-Head kept twisting away from them like a petulant child, shouting, "You fucker, I heard you singin. Awright. Watch this, fucker. That's,

you were singin, that's my song. Watch this, asshole. Tokyo ain't got shit," and he yelled over to Ox-Head, "A-1365!" then to me: Gimme that as he grabbed the mic out of my hand. A picture came up on the screen of a woman, totally naked this time, letting off balloons in a spa or something, the Fukusukes adjusted the angle of the screen to make it easier for Boss Baldy to see the words but he must've known them by heart because he didn't even glance at it, his eyes squeezed shut as he launched into some song about I don't care what kind of misery my spouse has to endure for the sake of my art, and my spouse knew that perfectly well when she married me, and what's more I'm determined to keep on with whatever wasteful extravagance and debauchery my art requires no matter how much she hates it in a horribly offkey croak, but there was more to come, slurred, moronic voices crying *eyyyy*, *Boss*, *woohoo* at the edge of my hearing suddenly tore through the gauzy fabric in the form of a middle-aged guy and his younger colleague in suits subtly plainer than those of the previous triumvirate, jumping in during lulls in Boss Sweaty-Head's song with slaphappy squawks of Hell yeah, Can't fuck with this guy, 'Sright muthafukkas, then they really let themselves off the leash, fondling the women's breasts and shoving their hands into their crotches, and though the triumvirate looked uncomfortable they didn't seem able to stop Sweaty and his two underlings, so they just chimed in, Yeah, Nice, Sing it. One of them was sitting directly beside me, a middle-aged guy in a suit the color of scum, enthusiastically clapping along and calling out Wow, yeah at Sweaty, off in whatever singsong dreamland he was currently inhabiting, but then the guy broke down momentarily and let out an *aaahh* that might have been a groan or just a sigh of exhaustion, I couldn't tell, before quickly recovering himself and bellowing, Yeah, sing it. Sweaty wasn't hearing any of it, though, he was completely absorbed, spastically flailing back and forth like a dying shrimp until the song finally ended and he exulted, Well? Who's the chump now? but as he turned to head back to his seat he stumbled, and when he put out his hand to steady himself on the table it capsized, spilling the ice bucket and the mineral water, the whiskey bottle, the glasses, everything, all over the floor, all the demons of hell were shrieking, it was literal pandaemonium, with Boss Baldy himself furiously screaming Hey, hey, which one of you fuckers tripped me? But before this volatile mixture could explode, a new and deafening sound reverberated through the room. Thinking quickly, Ox-Head had put on another song. She grabbed the mic and started singing.

And she was amazing. From a falsetto register she leapt suddenly down to a rumbling basso then ran back up the scale, describing a beautiful wave with her voice. She had full command of her vocal chords, and that voice, with its strange and subtle distortion, was filled with something like a chemical distillate of pure emotion. I got all choked up. So did the triumvirate. The threesome from Osaka were listening in wide-eyed silence. All the demons and rakshasas were enraptured. But then the sweaty boss blew his top again. Apparently he couldn't accept the idea of someone else winning over the crowd, and he started yelling, Hey, fucker, whaddaya think yer singin. I'm, I'm, my yer song, planting his hand on the upturned table to try and heft himself off the ground but only succeeding in falling flat on his ass, and while the suited triumvirate were flapping about trying to help him up he started in again screaming, "Fucker, what, whadda you think yer singin, just some fucking woman, fucker, you fucking ox," suddenly he's swinging at one of the rakshasas, the suited triumvirate trying to hold him back but too worried about offending him to do much good, so Sweaty's on an unfettered rampage, the one with the ox head seemed to be on the fence about trying to intercede so she just kept on singing with a flummoxed look on her face, but there was still more to come. A tall, thin-faced man in chunky black-rimmed glasses with the aura of a top-level bureaucrat came tottering in with the Fukusukes over by the TV. The one with the ox head promptly passed him the mic. Mr. Top-Level Bureaucrat looked startled for a moment but then manufactured a smile and started singing. I was impressed with the ox-headed one for getting the six suits out partying on the company dime to go back where they'd come from, but since they'd torn down the gauzy hangings when they barreled in, their spot was totally visible, that is, we were all sitting on the same elliptical black faux-leather sofa, and I was sitting directly beside one of the plainly dressed guys and the man in the scum-colored suit, close enough to rub elbows. The man let out another complicated *aaahh* and turned his hollow eyes towards me, saying in a low voice, "Hey. Freelancer, right?" and since it was too much work to explain I just answered Sure, something like that, which he apparently took as an invitation to start nagging me, I had to put up with him telling me, "I'm sure that seems alright to you now, but ever think about your future? Do you? You've got no security, do you?" Neither do you, buddy, I wanted to say but I held off, I just said Who knows, and gave him my best shit-eating grin, to which he replied, "I'm telling you. It's all very well for you right now, but you've got no security. Whenever I see some young guy who's on TV or something, I always want to ask him, what about the future? What'll you do?" Another *aaahh* and his hollow eyes turned toward Boss Shiny, acting as batshit crazy as ever, then fell torpid to the face of his watch. The bureaucrat was still singing with that smile plastered on his face, which really seemed to get Boss Baldy going again, he stood up and shouted, "Hey, you. Fucker. You call that a song? Yer total shit," thrusting his right arm out and pointing straight at Mr. Top-Level Bureaucrat, but he was in the bureaucrat's blind spot so this accusation went unnoticed, which made Bald-and-Sweaty even more indignant: "Hey, fucker, give it up already. What the fuck're you doin, hey," and in the middle of this tantrum he started throwing edamame, candy, strawberries, chocolates, crumpled up napkins, whatever he could get his hands on at Mr. Top-Level Bureaucrat. Ordinarily, in that situation I would've expected the middle-aged guy sitting next to me to try and stop Sweaty, and up till then that's what he'd been doing. But something must've snapped inside that scum-colored suit, because he started yelling, "Yeah, yeah. You suck, you fucking idiot," and plucking the edamame out of a bowl on the table in front of him to chuck at the bureaucrat. Things really snowballed from there. All three of the guys being wined and dined and all three of the guys doing the wining and dining started showering the bureaucrat with abuse accompanied by a hail of snacks and trash. Right then the third chorus of the song ended, and there was a short musical interlude. Expecting praise and applause but getting peppered with soybeans and garbage instead, Mr. Bureaucrat stopped smiling and turned livid, hollering What the hell, wh-what, what do you guys think you're doing, but then the next verse started and that smile was back on his face, singing, the hail of beans and trash becoming ever more violent, the bureaucrat clearly torn between his song and his rage, smiling and fuming in turn, until eventually one of the rakshasas couldn't bear it any longer and she switched off the song, dragging the bureaucrat back into the hidden depths of some other room.

Something must've set Sweaty and the suits off at that point because they started going fucking bananas, and when the dust finally settled, the St. Matthew Passion was wafting through the wreckage of the demolished bar. Some yakuza type had appeared out of nowhere and was ranting and raving about god knows what. Broken glass was scattered all over the floor. The girl with the horse's head vouched for me to the police, This gentleman had nothing to do with it, only she'd taken off the horse head and had a human face, and a few days later I went back to the panty bar to thank her for getting me out of that mess. The Setsubun party was over by then, all the girls were wearing their natural human heads, and this time nothing got crazy. After that I went to the panty bar seventeen times all told, and every time I asked specifically for Satoe the horse-headed girl. I even accompanied her in to work sometimes. Every time I went, it cost me somewhere between seventy and a hundred thousand yen. The money ran out before number eighteen, though, so nothing for it, I headed off to the last place in the world I wanted to go, which is to say the shop in Namikichō.

A young shop girl with golden hair was sweeping out front. Morning. Good morning. Though

I've seen better, know what I mean? And then into the shop. It was a grand place. Back when I was born it had been a rambling, old-fashioned china shop, in the family for generations, over the course of which the paper of the sliding doors had become stained with age, but now here it was in this new building, a modern showroom on the first floor with offices on the second, separated from the house behind it by a courtyard, the house itself a bright and elegant affair that unfolded into a third and then a fourth floor, a nice shop and a nice house and a nice building. Not to mention that they'd hired girls with hair every color of the rainbow—it was a hell of a place. A grand place. I also exchanged a Morning. Good morning. Though I've seen better, know what I mean? with the salesgirl in the showroom, her hair dyed slate grey. Climbing the white iron staircase in back, I only got as far as Morning. Good morning. with the industrious scarlet-haired shop girl. This particular young lady wasn't terribly sociable. So I got right down to business, which, isn't to say I gave her the whole spiel, just a brief question, The boss here?

To which she replied curtly, Nope, leaving me to wonder what to do. I had no desire whatsoever to wait for my mother in her office. But I also felt uncomfortable heading up, to the third floor, to the apartment my older sister had been eyeing like a hungry tiger but which our mother had doggedly denied her because she intended it for me once I was married, and I felt even more uncomfortable going up to the fourth floor, fitted out as it was for ease of living in solitary old age, so I told Scarlet, I'll be in the house, let me know when she gets back, pleiades. Sure, replied Scarlet without even a glimmer of a smile, and I walked the walkway across the hollow of the courtyard and into the house, that is, to the second floor living area, where I heated up some coffee in the kitchenette and sat gazing out at the plants in the courtyard as I drank it.

An imported luxury car like a massive white battleship. My mother backing into the garage.

"Sure, I know that, but I've been doing a lot of thinking myself," or some bullshit. You wanna know what I've been thinking about? Well, why do you work so hard, for one thing. I know you're convinced that however much you expand the company, I'll run it into the ground in no time flat if I get to do things my way. But the thing is, you're going to die before me, in which case I'll be president, and not just on paper. In which case the company really is gonna go under like you say, so why don't you quit racing around 24/7 all jazzed up and smothered in Chanel checking out hotels and wedding halls and just get some sleep already? Since it's just gonna go under anyway.

"Yeah. I know, I know. Well, I mean, sure." 'Tis just as you say—I'll end up as some low-rent entertainer. But, may I just say something in my defense? It's true, work isn't exactly my thing. But why do you think it turned out that way? Could it be that you never let me do anything around here because you always said I would fuck it up? Could that be it?

"Yeah. Sure. Yeah. Yeah. Uh huh, yeah." I figured I might as well try just nodding along with everything she said. When do people learn to do that, anyway? I don't think I got the hang of it till I was thirty or so. When I was younger I wasted so much time, fighting her every step of the way. And it didn't get me any closer to becoming what I wanted to be when I grew up. I never should've gone to an arts and crafts high school. Looking back on it, my dad didn't feel all that strongly about it either, he just kind of decided on a whim. Doing the design program was a mistake. His mother said sending Kitada to Hokudai had been a mistake, too, but Kitada had never said anything about that.

"Well. Well, you know. Uh huh. For today, well, for now that's, yeah. A loan. An advance, yeah, an advance, what was it, the May after next? An advance. Huh? You're not sure? Well, I guess that makes sense. OK then—hm? What's that? The house? Well, the rent doesn't amount to that much, so I might as well just keep on living there, but that's, well, next time I'll stay longer, but today I gotta, I'm a bit busy. Huh? You're kidding. For real? It's already set? You can't refuse? That's that? Aw c'monnnn. You could've at least talked to me first." The go-between and the two of us and one parent each. Five altogether, a formal dinner in formal dress. And I couldn't just eat in silence. I had to say something, whatever came out. It sounded hellish, but it was the price of the loan, so what could I do? With the advance on my allowance and the photograph of my prospective bride in hand, I headed to the panty bar. A budgie resting on the eaves flapped away into the sky.

One o'clock in the afternoon, standing on the traffic island watching a steady stream of people go by, the most numerous being young women in flimsy red and gold kimonos with countless tawdry accoutrements, all of them wearing hairpins from which dangle little tinkling gold-plated bells along with something white and fluffy wrapped around their necks, looking pleased as punch as they totter along in twos and threes, their mincing steps carrying them past me and through the doors of the train. Students are the next most common, most of them dressed pretty much the same: flannel shirts and jeans. The contents of their hulking backpacks are probably the same too, everything they might need in a pinch—books, maps, notebooks, dictionaries, guidebooks, walkman, headphones, contact solution, something to write with, spare batteries, that kind of stuff. They board the train, too, wearing looks of surprise or fear. Housewives are next. Here there's a variety. As soon as I think to myself People still wear those old-fashioned jackets? another one walks by wrapped head to toe in designer clothes, a few million yen on legs. Don't get on the train looking like that, I want to say. This one looks worn out. That one's bouncing along like a teenager. Zoned out. Inflamed. Like I said, a variety. Virtually nothing in common. Except that ten or twenty or thirty years ago, all of them were tottering along in their own cheap kimonos, bells tinkling in their hair. Can't say I understand it. Into the train they go. There aren't too many laborers or office workers around, probably because it's the weekend, so beggars are the next most numerous bloc, followed by musicians; they all crowd onto the train except for me, forever left behind.

I know perfectly well that I won't make it on time if I don't hurry up and get on a train, but Satoe still hasn't shown up. What's the deal, asking me for a loan then not coming to collect,

I was supposed to go with my mother and the go-between but I shook them off, handed them some bullshit about having to take care of something and got myself all the way out here, I mean come on, I check my watch and it's already been half an hour, I'm gonna be seriously late if I don't get going already. What can you do, she probably found some other client to sponge off, it sucks but fuck it, what can you do, I grabbed the brass railing of the green train that had just pulled up and heaved myself aboard. The facing bench seats are so close they're almost touching, and the poker-faced guy across from me is creeping me out. This is why I don't ride the train. But, the only place to get the bus for Lake Onokoro is a stop on this line. There are plenty of hotels right here in town, so why the go-between decided it was a good idea to use a hotel in the middle of nowhere I'll never know. Because it makes up for the hassle by being ever so gorgeous? But that means I have to sit here getting the stink eye from this stone-faced creep, like some Incan relic with his thick eyebrows and round eyes and round forehead. I can't stand it. I avert my eyes and twist my body into an unnatural position to look out the window, where houses line the track right up against the side of the train. They're all decrepit little wooden places, with verandas jutting out into cramped backyards. The train slows down, maybe out of consideration for the noise, and I can see TVs flickering blue in dim rooms beyond the verandas, exhausted old women, futons airing out, mikan growing on mikan trees, dirty cats taking sulky catnaps, I hate knowing there are Sunday afternoons even in these houses and these yards so I turn back to the inside of the train, and there it is again, that stark-naked gaze. That stark-naked poker face. What else can I do, I squeeze my eyes shut, and while they're shut the train starts to pick up speed, the scenery going from concrete and glass and iron to something more abstract, from which point on I stared fixedly out the window until suddenly everything outside went black. We'd entered a tunnel.

I got off the bus at the end of the line after a drive up winding mountain roads. The bus made a U-turn then drove off, farting out pitch-black smoke. Every particle of that smoke is settling into my lungs, isn't it, I thought, gazing out at the moldering scenery. There wasn't much to look at. The bus turnaround and the cliffs and the waiting area for the pleasure cruise. At the right time of year, I imagine there'd be at least a few tourists here for a cruise around the lake, but this was the off-season. The area was deserted, and the little souvenir stand next to the ticket office-slash-waiting area was shuttered. Graffiti on the shutters read, "Eradication of the mind. Our critique." Beyond it the surface of the lake, where I could see an observation tower thrusting up from the leaden waters into the low-slung sky.

A peeling metal signboard flapped in the wind. Sliding open the aluminum sash door, I stepped into the ticket office-slash-waiting area. The unnecessarily large print on the ticket machine read Lake Onokoro Pleasure Cruise (stopping at the Tower Pavilion) Adults 777 yen Children 333 yen. I fed a bill into the machine and bought a 777-yen ticket, hah! Me, an adult! then plopped down in one of the plastic seats to wait for the boat to arrive. I was supposed to've been there at three. An island castle, standing in the middle of the lake. Like a dream! A fantasy! they probably thought at first. But there was no getting around the fact that it was an abject failure. Sure, it was the off-season right now so what can you do, but the forlorn aura of the faded "Ice Cream" banner and the splintered reed screen rotting in the corner of the waiting room, the feeling that it was over, made it clear that even during tourist season no one was coming here, and the observation tower rising out of the lake—the fantastical island castle, that plan was obviously dead in the water. If this were a private enterprise, it would've gone belly up ages ago.

The boat arrived. YTIREPSORP DNA EPOH. Its name was written on the hull from right to left, the old-fashioned way. The overall tone was like a knockoff Donald Duck: the hull was a bird's head, the stern narrowed into tailfeathers, on the sides of the two-story cabin were pinwheels of various sizes, ooh a fairytale, and stripes of yellow paint had been slapped on here and there against the white background. That is to say, I felt like it had its own kind of unity, but with a stupa carved on the hull, monsters painted on the mainmast, and god knows why but gigantic sabers thrust in here and there, someone's vision had been realized directly, as is, with no foresight as to the result, producing an air of some fantastical oddity, who the fuck built this idiotic boat? Imagine the faces the workers at the shipyard must've been pulling. Pissed off, scowling. Or maybe they went about their work with earnest expressions on their faces. And what expression was I supposed to wear *riding* the damn thing?

Who knows. Crossing a bobbing pontoon bridge at the behest of some old guy gotten up like a fisherman, I boarded the YTIЯƎꟼꙄOЯꟼ ᗡИA ƎꟼOH.

I figured it might be nice to watch the tower approaching across the lake, so I left the cabin and climbed the iron stairs to a sort of observation deck. But despite the fact that there'd been no previous sign of it, a milky-white mist had descended during the few dozen seconds I was in the cabin, enshrouding everything, I could barely even make out the ticket booth on the other side of the bridge, when *braaaaaaaaaaanh*, *braaaaaaaaanh*, *papapaanh*, *babraanh*, with a series of moronic sounds the ship pulled away from shore. I felt like I was setting sail on Charon's ferry.

A Japanese restaurant. The window looking out over a courtyard. I wonder if they'd decided on regular chairs because sitting the traditional way is so uncomfortable. "Wasn't it a lovely boat?" Nitta Tomiko remarked. What part of that ridiculous boat could anyone possibly call lovely? That's the stupidest thing I ever heard. I think. I ponder. Though maybe it's just me, I'm the one who's being ridiculous. I think, fainthearted as ever. I think, as the moving strains of something in G-sharp minor pierce my heart, because the vast majority of the people in this kingdom really are morons, way more of them will swallow whatever bullshit doesn't leave a bad taste in their mouths, these idiotic pigs drunk on formulaic romance and trite fantasies, than would ever let themselves realize how ridiculous that boat was and be ridiculed and dismissed as cranks for even saying so, so I'll probably die alone and hopeless in the gutter, but sorry, ridiculous is ridiculous, and more important, what happens if I marry this idiotic pig Nitta Tomiko who thinks a boat like that is lovely? Our home becomes an exhibition hall for everything trite and formulaic, the two of us laughing at the TV, foolish lunches in neighborhood restaurants, eating strangely disheveled bento boxes. Not a fucking chance. I think, looking again and seeing that Nitta Tomiko is ugly. Stupid and ugly. Money is maybe her one redeeming quality. They made it clear that she's got plenty of it, and if her clothes and jewelry are anything to go by, there's no question she's the daughter of a very wealthy family indeed. But you know what, I'm the scion of a wealthy family too, and I haven't fallen so low that I'd marry someone as ugly as Nitta Tomiko for the sake of money. I'd sooner kill myself.

I thought, and, well, this is true of anything, but it's a lot harder to put things together than it is to smash them apart, so even though I'm already going to refuse, I might as well fuck things up so much that she'd never agree to it anyway, I thought, and then I did.

Which is to say, all I did was tell them exactly what kind of a person I am: That I spend all my free time at the panty bar. That I dropped out of high school. That I'm a spendthrift. That I've got my head in the clouds and I've never done an honest day's work in my life because I despise hard work. That's all. But the effect was instantaneous. Nitta Tomiko turned to stare vacantly out the window, Nitta Tomiko's mother glared at the go-between like she was about to lose her mind, the go-between recovered from his initial panic and tried to salvage the situation with an ill-considered belly laugh, and my mother started desperately gasping for breath like a dying fish. For the coup de grace, I pronounced, "Eel really is best when you slurp it this way, don't you think?" and, leaning my face down over the serving tray, I slurped at the pieces of broiled eel. But broiled eel isn't particularly easy to slurp; I thrust my tongue into the meat and broke off a piece, then pursed my lips and sucked it into my mouth, but you can't really eat eel without wanting some rice, so with my face still hovering over the lacquered box, I thrust my stiff fingers straight in and shoveled a handful into my mouth. Realizing that using my hands might be against the rules, I offered an exculpatory, Rice, you know? then hunched over again to suck up another piece of eel. Having sucked up about half of it like that, my mouth started to hurt, so somehow managing a straight face and a hearty voice, I repeated, "Ahh, that really is the most delicious way to eat eel. To say nothing of the liver in a nice eel-liver soup. Come on now, everyone, eat up," then replaced the lid on my food and took a swig of sake straight from the decanter. Nobody moved a muscle. Nor said a word. I felt suddenly exhausted and stopped talking. It was nearly five o'clock. The mood was too awkward for me to stay, so I grabbed a moist towelette and wiped away the rice that was stuck to my face, then stood up and excused myself, I'm off for a quick stroll, and stroll I did, around the courtyard of the Tower Pavilion. It was full of stone statues. An explanatory plaque said they were the work of a famous sculptor named Yoshida Yoshizō.

But the statues were truly strange, two girls maybe seven years old cocking their heads at a turtle on a tray; an office worker suffering from lumbago; a guy who looked like he might be the head of accounting pumping his fist; a sushi chef; beloved fishmonger Isshin Tasuke; a trendy teenage girl; a nurse, the courtyard was chockablock with statues of people generally unsuited to being the subject of sculpture. It couldn't have been more bizarre. Off at the edge of the courtyard stood a red torii. On the other side, a flight of moss-covered stone steps led up and out of sight. A yellow lamp hung there. A wooden sign, reading THIS WAY TO OBSERVATION TOWER. I went under the torii and up the stairs. Sure enough, at the end was the observation tower. I opened the heavy wooden doors and went in. A stairwell crawled up along the wall of the featureless, deserted atrium-like interior. Just inside the door, three candlesticks stood on a tray covered with wax drippings. Beside them, a wooden box with an opening like a bullet hole. Into which I put a coin, and lit one of the candles.

The stone steps reeked of mold, maybe because nobody ever used them, and I instantly regretted my decision. That sort of place looks nice from the outside, but there's nothing of interest when you go in, and even if I went all the way to the top it was already dark outside, not to mention the fact that in a mist like that I definitely couldn't expect to see much of anything to begin with. And yet, there's something pitiful about giving up and going back down once you've started. Might as well go all the way, so I gripped the dust-blanketed handrail and groaned my way up the tower. The room at the top was maybe a hundred feet square. When I went out onto the balcony it was just as I had expected, couldn't see a thing. Well there you go. Figured as much. I was about to go back down when I heard those moronic sounds echo out again, *braaaaaaaaaaanh*, *braaaaaaaaaaanh*, *papapaanh*, *babraanh*. A single beam of orange light pierced the mist. Boat must've just left, I thought. And then I got a bad feeling. I flew down the tower stairs in a panic, returned the candlestick to the tray, and ran down the stone steps and under the torii, cutting across the forest of stone sculptures on my way back to the lobby.

"That was the last boat of the day," a recently deceased concierge who bore a striking resemblance to Klaus Nomi informed me from where he sat behind the front desk in a lead-colored uniform. So nothing for it, I got a room at the Tower Pavilion, boarded the first ferry the next morning, then a bus, a train, and finally home. I felt sluggish and a little feverish, maybe because the room had been cold and I hadn't slept well, and I stayed in bed till nightfall. Then I read for a while. The nasty texture of the eel coiled in my stomach. I Klaus'd my eyes.

"So? How was the marriage interview?" asked Kizaki lightly, but, how the hell did he know about that in the first place? It really stuck in my craw, so instead of telling him anything about the interview itself, I asked, How'd you know about that? He seemed confused. "You told me about it yourself." But let me make this crystal clear, I hadn't told a soul about the marriage interview. Plus, I hadn't even seen Kizaki in six months, so how could I have told him?

"When?"

"What? You were talking about it just the other day."

"Where?"

"What do you mean where? Here." Kizaki seemed totally sure of himself, scanning the bright interior of the café before adding, "We were sitting in the same spot, even. You were right there in that chair, drinking apricot tea."

"Whaa? Like I'd ever drink apricot tea."

"I'm telling you."

"When was that again?"

"Friday, week before last, I think. Remember, you stopped in here on the way back from Yoshihara's opening?"

I remembered going to Yoshihara's exhibition. I'd left the house wearing dark brown pants I bought in Paris, and a black wool Nehru jacket I'd also bought in Paris.

A modern apartment building in a residential area. Long and narrow, with one unit on each floor. The fourth held the venue, at the top of a steep flight of stairs. A sea of people was thronging Yoshihara ten or twenty deep, I couldn't get close enough to talk to him even if I wanted to, so I figured I might as well check out the paintings instead. But I'd been underestimating them. I mean, they were Yoshihara's, after all, they wouldn't amount to much. Or so I thought, but as I looked from one to the next, I started to feel a little edgy. Irritated. They had something. I couldn't exactly pinpoint what it was, but I kept looking from one to the next in the hopes that the *something* was just my imagination, or, a mistake, or a happy accident, maybe. But I made it all the way around the room without finding anything to bolster that notion. As I stood looking at the last painting, some girls next to me were gushing to each other about how He's really got something, doesn't he. I was overwhelmed by a sense of defeat. This Yoshihara was someone I'd never really given the time of day. Even his own friends took it for granted that he was going nowhere, and back then anyone could see at a glance that his paintings were garbage, but these new ones were something else entirely. My belly got hot and my arms felt clammy. I looked around for someone I knew but there was no one. Not even a vague acquaintance. The one person I recognized was a comedian who hosted a daytime TV show, but even if I knew him, he didn't know me. The comedian was giving Yoshihara a big hug, congratulating him. A ring of hangers-on stood around them, grinning away. Then came the toasts, and I just stood there drinking beer after beer until I guess I finally bailed on the party without ever having said hello to Yoshihara. Outside it was pitch dark and pouring, and being a residential area, there wasn't a taxi or a rickshaw to be seen. I pelted through the darkness. But no matter how fast you run, you can't outrun the rain. Drenched is drenched. My 10,000-franc wool coat was sopping. When this kind of thing gets drenched, it's done for, I seem to recall telling myself miserably, Trashed, totally worthless, the light of the fluorescent lamps reflecting off the paint that covered the uniform green walls and pillars of the wooden station building.

"I'm pretty sure I went home early that night."

"Are you kidding me? You were totally out of control, just talking shit about Yoshihara the whole time."

"I was?"

"You were."

"But, don't you think Yoshihara's pictures had gotten better?"

"Nope, still garbage," Kizaki replied before I'd even finished.

"Yeah, they were, weren't they. Total garbage."

"Obviously."

"Were they, though?"

"They definitely were."

"Weird. You sure we're talking about the same day?"

"No question. Come on, it was Yoshihara's opening."

"And, I was drinking?"

"Until three."

"Jesus."

"It was a nightmare. You said you wanted ramen so we went to get some, and you were saying something about how ramen tastes best if you slurp it like this, then you stuck your face straight into the bowl."

"Huh."

"'Huh' my ass."

"But, the thing is..." I still wasn't convinced, but then Kizaki asked me again.

"So how was it? The marriage interview?"

"I did some stupid shit and they turned me down."

"What do you mean, some stupid shit?"

"Well, to the eel."

"You slurped it?"

"Maybe."

"Were you sober?"

"Maybe."

"I'd turn you down too," Kizaki said before lapsing into silence. I gave myself over entirely to watching the passersby outside the plate glass window. A guy wearing a sandwich board with an advertisement for a panty bar was getting tossed this way and that by the crowd, as listless as a corpse.

"Speaking of," said Kizaki.

"What?"

"Did you hear Yoshihara got married?"

"Yeah?"

"Yeah," said Kizaki, and then he told me the

name of the young woman Yoshihara had married. I blurted out a stupefied Hanh? so Kizaki said it again, enunciating every syllable this
time: “Nitta Tomiko.” Me: Horseshit, before the
words were out of his mouth.

I married Satoe a week later. My mother was
bedridden after hearing about Satoe’s background, but she finally recovered and started
pushing herself harder than ever at the store. Satoe quit her job to become a housewife. Instead
of moving into the house in Namikichō, we decided to make our home in the rented place in
Nigiwaichō where I was already living.

Three months later. Clothes and bread and
cups strewn about the three-mat room and the
four-and-a-half-mat room and the six-mat room.
Trash and anything else you could imagine.

I loathe all these ostentatious gadgets and ap-
pliances. Whenever I’m faced with one of these
grotesque, utilitarian contraptions—an automat-
ic fish grill, say—it seems to represent the em-
bodiment of my own petty desires (in this case
the desire to eat some grilled mackerel), and

then the coldness in my heart expands out to encompass my entire life, my soul ballooning with misanthropy and cynicism and endarkening my very existence. 'Swhy I'd been careful to get rid of everything but the bare essentials. But after Satoe moved in, suddenly a hairdryer; a foot warmer; a hot-water bottle; a sake warmer; all kinds of pots and pans; a mochi maker; wetsuits; helmets; hordes of stuffed animals; clothes for all seasons; half-used notebooks, pencils, felt-tip pens, ballpoint pens; magazines and antiquated books; an electric massager; plates, jars; radios and portable music players; candles; flashlights; ashtrays; cases for who knows what; baskets for god knows what; mysterious bits of cloth and paper; a bronze statue of a packhorse neighing into the void; a similarly bronze monkey; bundles of letters, postcards, photographs; a tube which seemed to contain her diploma, and all kinds of other mysterious miscellanea spread throughout the house, to the point that you literally can't set foot without stepping on something. In the great literatus Natsume Sōseki's novel *I Am a Cat*, the protagonist Mr. Sneaze's wife is described as "a woman so impoverished when it came to the concept of the appropriate place for something that she kept her expensive sugar in the bureau," and Satoe is precisely that kind of woman; previously, the three-mat room had been the bedroom, the four-and-a-half-mat room had been the living room, and the six-mat room was for entertaining guests, but at some point this inexorable wave of crap flooded them all in equal measure, so I'm constantly bewildered about why things are where they are, like yesterday for instance. I needed a pair of pants, so I unearthed one from the mountain of clothes and stuck my left leg through, only to encounter something vaguely sticklike when my foot reached the ground. Mystified, I finished putting on the pants then cleared away some underwear of mine, Satoe's socks, and some fabric of obscure purpose until lo and behold: a sickle, thrust into the tatami. Only I didn't remember thrusting a sickle into the tatami, in which case it must've been Satoe, but I couldn't even begin to imagine why the hell she might have thrust a sickle into the tatami, and frankly it gave me the creeps, I mean, I had never kept a sickle in the house before, which meant that the sickle and everything else had to be part of Satoe's trousseau, but she only brought one suitcase with her when she moved in, so when—*how*—did this vast collection of objects make its way into our house? It was a mystery.

It was dangerous to have a sickle thrust into the floor, though, so I immediately pulled it out and hid it under the porch, but that didn't answer the fundamental question of how the hell Satoe ended up thrusting a sickle into the tatami in the first place, like was Satoe cutting the grass in the yard and thought, Aaaaa, cutting grass is such a pain in the ass. How did I get stuck doing this shit? What a bummer. At this rate I was better off mixing scotch-and-sodas and singing karaoke at the panty bar. Fuuuuuck! then ran into the house sandals and all, swinging the sickle around all slick with sweat from working out under the sun, and the sickle slipped out of her hand and went spinning through the air and stuck into the tatami? Seems highly unlikely. There's no way Satoe would ever cut the weeds in the garden, too much work, and anyway, it's winter. There aren't any weeds in the garden for her to cut.

In which case what could she have been doing? Sickle dancing? Aaaaa, sickle dancing is such a pain in the ass. How did I get stuck doing this shit? Bare-breasted with this cloth wrapped around my waist, I feel like Ame no Uzume no Mikoto. And what am I even supposed to do? Swing the sickle around like this? Then what? Waggle my hips, right? Ahaha, this is actually kind of fun. Sickle dancing, who knew. Ahaha, wheeee! and while she was dancing around flailing the sickle, bopping so energetically that she was slick with sweat even though it's winter, the sickle slipped out of her hand and went spinning through the air and stuck into the tatami? Definitely not. Dancing's a little too abstract a pursuit for Satoe, and anyway, there's no such thing as sickle dancing.

In which case I have to admit that it truly baffled me how Satoe ended up thrusting a sickle into the tatami, but even more baffling has been Satoe's transformation. It's like she's become a different person. First off, in her panty bar days Satoe was kind of skinny, but in the past three months she's ballooned to twice her old size. And it isn't just that she's put on weight; it's a bizarre kind of inflation, I, guess you could say, her face ballooning out like a rubber ball, her nose and eyes swallowed up by the bulging flesh, her features completely altered, leaving not even a vestige of her former beauty, that is, her eyes and nose are blockaded with flesh and she's become nothing but a hideous lump of meat. And with her body ballooning up like that, I guess changing her clothes and whatnot must have become too much of a hassle, because at night she'll sometimes drape a ruddy brown bathrobe kind of a thing around her shoulders, but apart from that she just sits around in her underwear all day long, and not underwear like when she worked at the panty bar, something more like a chemise, and because she never goes out to do any shopping or anything, I haven't seen her actually get dressed in over a month.

Naturally, with Satoe in that state, at first it was endless fights and arguments.

"Hey dumbass, clean up a little, will you?"

"Who're you calling a dumbass, dumbass?"

"Shut up, dumbass."
"You're the only dumbass here."
"No, you're the dumbass."
"Shut *up* already, you dumbass!"
"Waaaah, quit it! Boo-hoo-hoo..."

But after a while the fights petered out. Maybe all that extra flesh squeezed her mouth shut, or cut off her windpipe or something, but either way she started saying less and less, and on the rare occasions when she did say something it was always muttered under her breath, and even if I asked her to say it again she wouldn't respond, so it never amounted to anything you could call a conversation, let alone a fight.

This state of affairs has me totally depressed. So lately I've been thinking about going to the old town to have some fun, you know, chase the blues away, but I couldn't pay off my credit card last month so now it's frozen, and I can't get another advance, which only makes me more depressed. Two in the afternoon. I stood up and threw on my wool coat, mushy and shapeless thanks to the drenching it had gotten, and told my wife, "I'm gonna go to Namikichō for a minute." No response. Just an almost imperceptible sideways wobble of the head. Heart swaying in the wind. I made for the front hall, picking my way across the mess littering the floor. Motes of dust floating in the air.

The golden-haired shop girl was talking to a customer, Welcome, with a slight bow and I went right past her, but when I said Hey to the grey-haired shop girl, she giggled and seemed to be blushing; I wondered what was up and when I looked at her something seemed different, so I looked again to try and figure out what it was, and her formerly grey hair was now white. Wow. That's quite a change. Teeheehee. And off she went. I headed up to the second floor and asked the scarlet-haired girl, She here? and got the usual perfunctory Yes. Would it kill you to be a little more courteous? I went into the living room at the rear of the second floor. Uncle Kudai's hulking frame was sunk into the couch as he leaned forward over the coffee table, leafing through some documents. Next to him, my mother seems tiny. His size makes the scale all screwy. Makes

Mom look like a leprechaun.

"Hi Uncle Kudai."

"Mm. Been awhile. Doing OK?" Uncle Kudai laughed, ledger never leaving his hand. I laughed too. So did Mom. But then Uncle Kudai's gaze dropped right back to his ledger, my mother dummied up, and I couldn't be the only one laughing so I returned to my usual expression of cool indifference, adopting the matter-of-fact, nothing matters air of someone who was only there because they'd asked him to come, and dropped into a chair by the patio.

Uncle Kudai pored over the documents, tapping away at his calculator and periodically asking my mother about something or other, listening to her quiet replies and patting himself on the back of the head with his open palm, clearing his throat uhum, ahem.

Previously. I had heard Uncle Kudai tell my mother in one of his merrier moods that They call me a monster in this business. Which wasn't necessarily Uncle Kudai blowing smoke, I had in fact seen a newspaper article to the effect that Uncle Kudai had been appointed president of a food distributor that turned over twenty billion yen a year, and that in a little over a year the company had grown rapidly, profits going through the roof, after two years their stock had gone OTC, and in the third year they had merged with the second-biggest company in the business, with Uncle Kudai installed as VP. Which is why it was awkward, laughable, ridiculous to solicit his opinion regarding the management of a little china shop that didn't even do ten million in yearly sales. The thing is, women are weak-minded, for the most part, and since, when dad died and mom had no choice but to take over the business she reorganized things on Uncle Kudai's advice and everything went swimmingly, I imagine she figured she'd just come to him for help again. It had to be a pain in the ass for Uncle Kudai, Mom always coming to him for advice like that, and what's more, going to a big man like him about a tiny business like this one was already terribly provincial, or...shameful. Embarrassing. My expression became more and more composed.

Hopeless, Uncle Kudai muttered. Huh? Does he mean me? Mother hung her head. "Should've shut this down a long time ago." Uncle Kudai was normally kind and genial towards us, but occasionally you'd catch a look in his eye cold enough to freeze your blood.

In the evening, my older sister showed up. Mom ordered an extravagant meal from a caterer, and the two of them laid it out on the table of our modern dining room. Uncle Kudai filled the lulls in the conversation with a constant stream of jokes, smacking the back of his head all the while, and went home after precisely three cups of sake. As he was leaving, he whispered a few quick words in my mother's ear, then to me he said, See you. You're gonna need to get your act together, you know, and climbed into his car.

Once Uncle Kudai was gone the atmosphere in the living room descended into wretched gloom, you couldn't help but be depressed by it, so before the talk turned heavy I stood up with a See you later, took the little bit of money I'd gotten and went to spend a little bit of time at the panty bar, and by the time I got home it was already after two. I got undressed and, out of regard for the supposedly sleeping Satoe, quietly crept into the three-mat bedroom, whereupon she mumbled, "Dumisdeal." I blurted out, "What? What does that mean?" but Satoe didn't answer. A momentary sensation of freefall, then nothing.

"The thing I appreciate most, that I value most highly, is your...rebellious spirit, I guess you'd say? Your rejection of all authority and whatnot. It seems to me that sort of thing runs consistently through all of your work. Do you think you could speak to that?" A newspaper reporter with a shoulder bag, taking notes as he interviews a grinning Yoshihara. Beside them an ice sculpture & lavish spread. But the reporter only has eyes for his subject, craning his neck further and further toward Yoshihara's face as he waits for an answer. Yoshihara, dressed to the nines and definitely *not* wearing a mushy wool coat, chuckles amiably, and begins, Hmm, dripping with self-confidence, then continues, "Hmm, I suppose maybe I do have a rebellious spirit that rejects all authority. Since that sort of thing does run consistently through my work." Nodding enthusiastically, the reporter scribbles in his notebook without ever looking down at his hands. But what the hell is there to scribble? Yoshihara just regurgitated his question word for word, and anyway, it was all bullshit to begin with. People who reject authority don't generally submit their artwork to juried exhibitions, do they?

Yoshihara was always savvy. Even back in elementary school. So he was always popular with the teachers and the girls, always getting picked to be class president and team captain. Where's the rebellious spirit in that? Yoshihara's paintings had been mediocre all along, and he never showed even a glimmer of talent. I was the one who did, and I can prove it: when it came time to make our fifth-grade yearbook, I was the one everybody nominated to do the illustrations. But Yoshihara fucked me then, too. The teacher had made him yearbook editor, and when he saw all the girls swooning over my drawings, it stoked the fires of his envy. So the bastard used his power to deep-six my illustrations. But not in an authoritarian way, oh no, it was all, Mm-hmm. Good. Really good. I'm very impressed. One thing does bother me, though, doesn't this cow's head look a little off? Thoughts? Yes, Kitagawa Sumiyo, go ahead. Mm-hmm, I agree. It does, now that you mention it. Right? I do think it looks a little off, but Aoyama Miyuki, what do you think? You think it looks a little off, too. Mm-hmm. I see. Well, there you go. I see. So I'm hearing a general consensus that this cow's head definitely looks a little off. I'm sorry, but do you think you could redraw it for us? and on and on, cleverly molding public opinion and creating a situation in which, if I refused to redraw it, everyone would think I was being self-righteous. Pretty despicable for a fifth-grader. It was only natural that I became despondent after having to swallow a whole series of these rejections and ended up dashing off some sloppy, obviously half-assed drawings. But when I delivered them to Yoshihara, he pretended to be thrilled, Mm-hmm. Now this is good. This is the stuff, and he gave them the OK on the spot, without even consulting Kitagawa Sumiyo and Aoyama Miyuki, who by this point were occupying a role somewhere between his secretaries and his personal assistants. The general evaluation of my art went down like the Hindenburg after that, Yoshihara teeheeheeing all the while. I wanted to ask the reporter Hey, Mr. Reporter, where's Yoshihara-the-rebel in all that? People were bowing and exchanging pleasantries all around me, while the ones who weren't stood vaguely on the fringes with a plate in one hand and a fork in the other, spaghetti dangling out of their mouths. No familiar faces, just like before, while in the center of the hall a pretty gorgeous woman in a pricey-looking kimono stood surrounded by a crowd of people. The reporter kept on asking questions, just like before.

"Now, it seems to me that your piece *Adolescent Jeunesse* is a direct expression of your thoughts on modernity. How does that strike you?"

"Hmm, yes, my piece *Adolescent Jeunesse*, takes, well, adolescent youth, or youthful adolescence you might say, and, hmm, I guess you could say the piece is a direct expression of my thoughts on this thing we call modernity."

Bwaaah. Bwaaah. Bwaaah. Three unpleasant, metallic squawks from somewhere to the right and behind me, and when I turned to look, a man in a cheap-looking tux was saying something into the microphone. The sound was terrible, though, and his voice kept frizzling into a sort of skweeskree sound: skweeskree the 49th skweeskree ... skweeskree is ... in commemoration SKWEEskree ... skweeskree last year's ... Mr. and Mskweeskree Kokeno Ichinen ... bring SKWEESKREE the auspicious crane and tortoise SKWEESKREE ... pleaSKWEESKREE ... so it was impossible to tell what he was saying. SKWEE. SKREE? What the hell is that all about, anyway? I wondered, when all of a sudden from behind the sort of stage at the front of the hall where the guy with the mic was standing and where Yoshihara was now seated beside some other VIP types even though I never saw him get up there, eight young women in pink suits emerged, all of them tall but horribly emaciated, bent at the waist and straining to wheel out giant—though then again they were fairly small, maybe three feet across—taiko drums, arranging them in the proper places and kneeling down to lock the casters, whereupon eight extravagantly muscular young men with bubble-butts bulging from their loincloths came flying out from the right side of the stage, sticks in hand, each one striking an exaggerated pose in front of his appointed drum, and for a while a mixture of hectic high tones and tones low enough to move your bowels thundered through the hall. It was too fucking loud to even wonder what the hell kind of entertainment this was supposed to be. I could feel my brain rattling around inside my skull, making me stupider, when a man and woman who seemed like a married couple got up on stage where the MC had been standing earlier and started reading a poem in a kind of call-and-response duet.

First, in a voice full up with emotion, the man recited,

I am the heart's turtle
The lonely heart's turtle
The sky over Yakutsk
Beneath that leaden sky
A crane upon the tundra stands

at which point the woman, raising her face at a forty-five-degree angle and forcing a sorrowful expression, cried out plaintively, "A crane upon the tundra!" complete with gesticulations, then kept repeating "A crane upon the tundra" over and over again like a backup singer. After she had repeated "A crane upon the tundra" four times, the man began intoning his poem once more:

Man: What does it mean to the crane
Woman: A crane upon the tundra
Man: that I am a turtle?
Woman: A crane upon the tundra
Man: 'Pon Thousand Year Hill, does the crane feel
Woman: A crane upon the tundra
Both: the sighing breath of Nirvana?

This last they sang in a tragic unison, repeating "The sighing breath of Nirvana" four times altogether, after which it was the man's turn to repeat "The sighing breath of Nirvana" while the woman took her solo.

Woman: The crane lives a thousand years, ten thousand years the turtle

Man: The sighing breath of Nirvana

Woman: Urashima Tarō reached the ripe old age of three thousand

Man: The sighing breath of Nirvana

Woman: The frail trees' branches brush the wise man

Man: The sighing breath of Nirvana

Woman: The sky of endless ages, ready-made frozen earth

Man: The sighing breath of Nirvana

Both: A lost balcony

The cacophonous drumming persisted throughout, but contrary to the rapturous intoxication of the performers themselves, the reactions of the crowd, mostly possessed of standard sensitivities like myself, seemed to generally fall into one of four categories: 1) What the hell is going on?; 2) This is ludicrous; 3) I can't bear to look; and/or 4) This is giving me the creeps, and even the people who felt obliged at first to at least pretend to be listening were now piling their plates with food or seeking out acquaintances and greeting them in hushed tones, the hall slowly filling with the murmur of voices. But the people on stage were so caught up in what they were doing that they didn't notice, they just kept on going as they had been, *Man*: Sgt. Pepper's band *Woman*: A lost balcony *Man*: smashed the folly of the conservative reactionary elements *Woman*: A lost crane continuing their absurd performance, and once the audience realized that the couple up on stage weren't paying any attention to them, they stopped paying any attention to the couple up on stage, striking up normal conversations and laughing at each other's jokes, and because the drums were so loud, everyone had to talk in big booming voices to be heard over the clamor, shouts and idiotic guffaws mixing with mournful wails about lost turtles and wild, machine-gun drumming, until the atmosphere finally reached the level of an Obon celebration at a reformatory, Mardi Gras in a lunatic asylum, and I started to feel like my head was going to explode. To gauge how noisy the hall really was, I tried letting out a Russian battlecry in a voice lowish though still loudish compared to a normal conversation: УРААА. No one even glanced my way. In fact, my shout was veritably swallowed up by the voice of some old cueball with bulging eyes and a unibrow gushing to his interlocutor, "But that wife of Yoshihara's, now there's a woman." So, loud as it was in there, I raised my voice a little more this time and tried calling out, "Yoshihara's wife is a babe." But just as before, no one could hear me over the sound of the drums, the bubbling cauldron of conversation, and the moronic recitation *Man*: An invoice swaying in the wind *Woman*: Their guarantee, only three thousand yen My experiment concluded, I thought to myself, Would you look at that, this place is as noisy as a rock club, but even as I thought this, what the old guy had said—about Yoshihara's wife being a babe—started to bother me. If what Kizaki had told me was true, then Yoshihara's wife should be Nitta Tomiko, my decidedly un-babely prospective bride from the observation tower. But that didn't make sense. I didn't see Nitta Tomiko anywhere. I scanned the room, wondering what the hell was going on, and what was going on seemed to be that every single woman in the place had been intentionally selected for her unattractiveness, the sole exception being that woman in the kimono, and from the way she was staying by Yoshihara's side and nodding to all the people clustered around him, she had to be his wife. Ergo, she must be Nitta Tomiko. But she couldn't be, Nitta Tomiko could never be a wonderful woman like that, in which case Yoshihara wasn't actually married to Nitta Tomiko, right? Right, not a chance. And yet...the pattern on that kimono did look familiar, somehow.

"УРААА, УРААА," I was basically screaming at the top of my lungs at this point, but the voice of the young man behind me was somehow worlds louder as he said, "That Nitta Tomiko could make any man famous," before bursting into a guffaw. УРААА. But it couldn't possibly be true. Let's get real, regardless of whether the marriage actually would've gone ahead or not, there's no way I would slurp eel in front of a woman like that. Man, I really don't get it, but now that you mention it, she looks... "УРААА.

УРААА. УРААА."

The performance had reached fever pitch, the drumbeat becoming ever more frantic, flams exacerbating the sense of urgency and spurring on the couple's recitation to its climax, screaming as they sobbed and wailed,

Man: In a noisy tavern *Woman*: The crane thus smashed *Man*: The turtle thus burst *Woman*: We two, crane and turtle, reduced to powder *Man*: The grains thrown *Woman*: into the crucible *Man*: Into the crucible *Both*: Into the crucible *Both*: Into the crucible and as I listened I peered at Yoshihara's new bride, jumbled thoughts and anxieties welling up suddenly to fill my mind, my heart, until I started to feel like I was going crazy, thank god it was so noisy in the hall, I let out three throat-rending screams to dispel this mounting feeling, УРААА. УРААА. УРААА.

The performance must have ended at some point. Everyone was staring at me. It was too awkward for words. But it would've been just as awkward to suddenly stop, so in a quiet voice I muttered another УРААА, small and forlorn. I could see a tall man in a uniform with two rows of gold buttons down the front striding toward me across the room, so I hurried to the exit. After I'd made it out of the hall, I glanced back over my shoulder. Yoshihara's wife was watching me. Our eyes met. Was it Nitta Tomiko after all? Even as this question passed through my mind, the flip phone in my pocket rang, which it almost never does. Struggling to open it, I barreled into a phone booth and when I finally managed to hit ANSWER, sure enough, it was Satoe. She spoke in what was, for her, an unusually clear tone, her voice low and neutral.

"Your mother died. Please get to Namikichō as soon as you can."

УРААА.

In spite of how young he was, the guy from the funeral parlor my sister and her husband had called acted all fucking worldly, with his shaved head and his quiet voice. Which maybe comes with the territory, but I could tell from his eyes and the way he talked that outside of work he was overflowing with vitality. Not that he gave the impression of being a cheery youth, far from it—it was a darker vitality he overflowed with, a melancholy potency, if he were a fish he would be a red snapper. Which is to say a one-note vitality, without any shades of gray, so no, the vitality of this Inō or whatever wasn't that kind of sniveling vitality, he was more like a flounder, yeah, exactly like a flounder that usually lies unsettlingly flat against the ocean floor but for whatever reason happens to be undulating along happily through the water just at the moment. And Inō's melancholy powers of perception must've seen through to my true fecklessness, because at first he kept coming reverentially to me with questions, but gradually he stopped and just started consulting with my sister or brother-in-law instead, so I had nothing to do, which is pretty much the same as saying I was just dead weight, and all my relatives were looking at me like I mean really, forced to scrape by with just the one maid after she lost her husband, and now this is how she ends up, what a pity, I mean really, the eldest son is such an idiot, nothing but trouble, apparently they found a gorgeous bride for him but the moron acted like a wild animal at the marriage interview and they turned him down, so out of desperation he married a girl from an amateur cabaret. I think she's over there somewhere. Oh, you mean her? Let's make sure to get a good look at her later on. I do wonder what a girl from an amateur cabaret would be like. Anyway, it must've been terrible for her with a son like that. And now she's dead. What'll become of the business? which made me want to come back with a shitty Mmmmmmm that may be so. Maybe what I did wasn't so laudable, but who the fuck are you to say anything about it? Plus they don't even call them amateur cabarets anymore! But it wasn't the time or place for that, and they hadn't actually said anything out loud, I could just see it in their eyes, so it's not like I could give them a piece of my mind, I simply hung my head in silence and went to sit in the mid-century modern easy chair in the shadow of the cabinet by the doorway to the kitchen, observing the mourners come and go. It was like a silent film. The usually lifeless void of the sprawling living room was filled with people sitting on every available surface, drinking and exchanging greetings and expressing their condolences to my sister and her husband. I watched everyone pursing their lips like monkeys, trying to look appropriately melancholy, gesticulating and flapping their gums, She seemed so lively only the other day, I simply don't know what to say, please try to keep your spirits up, Yes of course, that's right, I saw her just the other... Mm-hmm. Mm-hmm. Ah, well. It's just, still and all, for this to happen. It really must be because her son is such a fucking idiot, and as I watched, the already faint reality of my mother's death faded even further, so I tried saying it out loud, quietly murmuring Maman died today. Feels kind of good, Maman died today. Suddenly I wanted to drink some sake, not this fucking café au lait. But the bottles of sake were in the middle of the room, and if I flounced in from my spot on the sidelines, I knew I would have to endure another cloudburst of condolences, with a healthy smattering of censure.

Once during a cloudburst I decided to go out for a stroll without an umbrella and got soaked to the skin. It was the middle of the night and the streets were deserted, and I stood there primordially drenched in the circle of light from a mercury-vapor lamp. I wanted a cigarette, but when I pulled them out of my pocket they were completely sodden inside the cellophane, totally unsmokable. I tossed the whole pack onto the ground, and it was carried away on the river of water sluicing through the street until finally it disappeared from sight. I need a smoke at all costs, I thought. If I give up on smoking now, I might as well give up on life, I thought. To smoke a cigarette in that circle of light in the middle of a downpour. That is my karmic duty, my cross to bear, I thought.

I got some cigarettes from a nearby vending machine. As long as I didn't break the seal, no rain could get in. The real problem, however, was a light. The lighter in my pocket was all wet, and the flint wouldn't spark. Which meant my only choice was to buy a new one, but it was the middle of the night, not mention the fact that it was torrentially raining, and there wasn't the glow of an open shop to be seen. I wandered aimlessly. There was nowhere to buy a lighter. My clothes were so saturated with rain that I might as well have been walking underwater. A lost cause? Am I a lost cause? The hobgoblins of my little mind were kicking up a ruckus so I took shelter inside the station, leaning against the wall where the ticket machines stood in ranks, reflexively wiping water from my hair and arms.

I hadn't really thought about it while I was out there getting pounded by the rain, but once I was under a roof it made me that much more aware of how wet I was, and I asked myself, What the hell is the point of this? It's ridiculous! Wouldn't it be better to give it up right now and go back to your nice warm house for a leisurely smoke? But just as I had decided to cut short my righteous mission and head home, I found a red lighter under one of the ticket machines, with a sticker that said MADOKA in fat, old-fashioned script over a scarlet chrysanthemum. Divine providence. A godsend. I renounced the change of heart I'd just had and picked up the lighter. Then I retrieved a scrap of cloth and a white plastic bag from the trashcan, put the cigarette pack and lighter into the bag, and cinched it shut before heading back out of the station. The women on the posters were eyeing me strangely. Quit looking at me like that.

I bowed my head, staving off the rain with the back of my own skull. Even so, between my wet fingertips and the water dripping from my hair and nose, the cigarette started to droop, but I nevertheless gritted my teeth against an unpleasant stench wafting through the circle of light and wiped off my fingers with the rag I'd picked out of the trashcan, finally managing to light the damn thing and get in three good puffs before it was done for, tossing away the sodden stub that, up till then, I'd been handling with such care, good riddance to bad rubbish, then hurrying out of the halo of light. I felt like I'd pulled it off. I felt like I'd somehow been spared. But I hadn't been spared. Maman died today. The shop would go under. But what I felt now was something like what I'd felt then. If I couldn't get a drink of sake right now I would be cursed for life, and yet, venturing out into the middle of the room was... As I was agonizing over this quandary, the familiar face of the white-haired shopgirl appeared, carrying a tray loaded with teacups past me into the kitchen. I stood up and followed.

Why is this girl always giggling, but, anyway, maybe I can get her to bring me some sake. The white-haired girl said, Oh, sure, and without even having to brave the living room, she filled a green teacup for me from a bottle of daiginjō that was sitting right there in the kitchen. Thank you. Teeheehee. Thank you. Teeheehee. Uh huh. Just leave it there. I'll pour for myself. Oh, are you sure? You sure?

My eyes lingered on the girl as she hurried in and out of the kitchen, going about her work, Wow, never seen her all in black before, I drank three cups, and Now I've had some sake. Maman died today. What do I do now? It's OK, don't worry about it. For now, just focus on the sake. He who chases two hares catches neither. I sat down on a stool and gave myself over wholeheartedly to drinking.

Me: "Hm?" The girl: "Hm?"

"What is it?"

"Did you say something just now?"

"Did I?"

"Yes. Something about Maman, or..." She'd heard me. But so what? There's nothing strange about it. All I'd done was put into slightly different words the fact that my mother had died. I gulped down my sake, and, "This is what I said: Maman died today." I drew out the Maman died today part, in a tragic tone redolent of that couple's recitation; the white-haired girl hung her head, and her shoulders started to tremble. She held the tray against her belly in anguish, and I guess it got so she couldn't even keep herself upright anymore, because she crumpled to the ground, trembling in apparent agony. Her white hair had come loose and was covering her face, obscuring her expression. When I squatted down to ask, Are you OK? it apparently pushed her over the edge, because she let out a Pffff and, no longer able to hold back, began hooting with uncontrollable laughter. She'd abandoned the tray at this point, holding her belly, tears streaming down her face as she writhed on the floor, and you know? She didn't look half bad. But how would this seem to everyone out in the living room? They'd be gossiping, no question, That boy is up to something strange again. He's yukking it up in the kitchen with one of the shopgirls. That fucking lech, what an embarrassment. I put my left arm around the girl, and with my right hand I covered her mouth. Her warm body convulsed in my arms.

"Let's go somewhere," I whispered into her ear. The strength left her body momentarily and I relaxed my arms, whereon the white-haired girl got to her feet and stood glaring down at me there on the kitchen floor. "Your eyes are the eyes of a dead fish. You are defilement incarnate. Do not touch me. Do not speak my name. You are cursed to spend all the days of your life caught between fear and disgrace. Begone, dissembler. Begone, interloper."

I. Don't know what to say.

Ash gets in your eyes. A flake got in my eye. When I got home from the crematorium, I turned on the television and the title *Now, Villager* came boioioinging onto the screen. A man and woman standing in front of some nondescript rural harbor started yammering away: "Now, Villager. And today we bring you to the village of Udai in Ōuji Prefecture. As always, we're your guides, Saruta Gento," "And Daitai Iyoko!" Picking up one of the foul-looking steamed buns that were neatly arranged on a plate beside them, Saruta exclaimed, "Wowww, so, wow, this is the local delicacy, is it? Beggar's buns? Well, 'scuse me for a moment, I'm just going to take a little bite, wow. Blech. Uh, that is, fascinating, you can really taste the local culture," at which Daitai Iyoko put on an exaggerated pouty face and gave him a playful little shove. "Sarutaaa, you can't dig in yet, we've got a special guest on the show todayyy." Pounding himself in the chest with an Mmgorrygorry, Saruta spluttered, "Oh, of course, of course. Today we've invited a wonderful guest to join us," then called out, "Mr. Yoshihaaara." The camera cut away to Yoshihara, standing in someone's front yard.

"Yes, hello, this is Yoshihara," responded Yoshihara. Then Daitai's voice, in the stilted tone of someone reading off cue cards: Mr. Yoshihara, recent recipient of the Gölmar Prize, is one of Japan's leading painters, whose work is held in high esteem both at home and abroad, after which Saruta cut in without a moment's pause to ask in a shrill voice, "And where are you right now, Mr. Yoshihara?"

"Hi, Yoshihara again. At the moment I'm in Udai village, at the workshop of a potter who produces a now extremely rare type of ancient patterned urn." The camera zoomed out to reveal a shabby fellow with long hair and a big beard standing next to Yoshihara, stopping once they were both in the frame. "This gentleman is the ceramic artist Fusai Kunio," Yoshihara explained, to which Saruta, seemingly unable to control his enthusiasm, responded with a vigorous Uh huh, Uh huh, followed by an impressed whistle from Daitai.

Yoshihara began a prefab interview with Fusai, who sighed like a man who had tried to make it as a musician. Then edited a magazine, then ran a record label. Then worked as a systems engineer. But nothing came of any of it, so now here I am, wearing *samue* and working as a potter. Fusai was obviously nervous, like he hadn't been in front of a camera since his guitar playing days, and to distract from this, he just acted like the whole thing was a huge imposition. A greenhorn like Yoshihara had no idea what to do with such a grumpy subject, of course, and the interview never got off the ground.

"No one really makes this kind of ancient patterned urn anymore, do they?"

"Nope."

Crickets.

Some old geezer in a peach cardigan was standing around in the background, staring at the camera with a dunderheaded look on his face.

"So do you really make this pattern by winding the rope around the pot like this?"

"Not like that, no."

"Oh, I see. Then how's it done?"

"Different ways."

"Oh, different ways, you say?"

"That's right."

Crickets.

Six yapping Pomeranians came bounding into the frame at that point, shaking off and sniffing around Yoshihara's feet then going wild, barking and yipping, one of them even putting its paws around Yoshihara's thigh and humping away, at which Yoshihara started groaning and yelping, Aiyaiyai, nonono, unhhh, and the already wobbly interview fell apart completely.

That was the last straw, and the camera cut back to Saruta and Daitai, who had relocated to a sandy beach while Yoshihara was interviewing Fusai. They were helping the locals haul in a fishing net. "Wow, I mean, heave-ho. What in the world could be in here?"

"I can't wait to find out!"

"We'll grill up all the fish in this here seine and have ourselves a feast."

"Too bad, Mr. Yoshihara, looks like you'll be missing out!"

They brought up the beach seine and the camera displayed the contents. But in place of the glittering fish they had anticipated, the net was full of resin bottles labeled in what looked like Russian. Chunks of concrete. Garbagey seaweed. "Ayaiyai. Nonono. Uuuunh. What's all this?" groaned Saruta, "Well, I wonder where

Mr. Yoshihara is now. Let's find out," and desperately began calling out, "Mr. Yoshihara. Mr. Yoshihaaara."

For his part, Yoshihara had relocated to the grounds of a temple while Saruta and Daitai were hauling in the seine. His breathing was ragged, as if he'd had to sprint to get from one place to the other in time.

"Huff. Huff. Huff. At the mo–huff–moment, I'm, um, I'm, um, where are we again? Right, a temple. Huff huff, I'm at a, a temple..."

"What temple is it?"

"Let's see, what was it called again... Well, it's a temple, anyway."

"Is it called Kukumanji?"

"Right, yes, that's it."

"And what sort of temple is it?"

"Let me see, what was it, it's...um, it's famous for..."

"Is it famous for its statues?"

"That's right, yes."

"And it's also known as the Temple of the Statues, isn't it?"

"I believe so, yes."

Behind Yoshihara, who was so out of breath that he'd forgotten the script and everything else, an odd-looking old crone was racing through her daily pilgrimage at a blistering pace. She was galloping around the grounds of the temple in a shabby kimono. Her hair in disarray. She looked vaguely familiar. I squinted at her, wondering what the hell she might be praying for, and the cameraman must've noticed her too, because the camera really seized on her. In that moment, the galloping old crone turned and shot a piercing look my way, croaking, "I guess it was a mistake to let him go to Hokudai after all."

Suddenly it's dark outside. The living room glows blue in the light of the television. I sit there motionless, late into the night.

I went to the supermarket to buy some tofu, and not the 380-yen Shinosuke stuff I usually buy, but some of that 70-yen injection-filled tofu that's been industrially smooshed into every nook and cranny of its square, white, plastic container. Turns out it really is a little different. To wit, Shinosuke tofu is produced to exacting standards using only naturally occurring magnesium chloride and so forth, I don't really know, but I saw once on *Now, Villager* how they let each individual block of tofu bob in a special tank of water, whereas this injection-molded stuff uses a gelling agent to help it fill the container completely, no water necessary, so when you want to get the tofu out of the package, you have to peel off the clear cover then turn the container upside down and make a slit in the bottom with a kitchen knife, which lets air get in between the plastic and the tofu.

The bamboo pattern stamped into the bottom of the carton had transferred itself to the block of tofu. And, no surprise given the price, the injection-filled stuff tasted awful. Though, that was only because I'm used to eating Shinosuke all the time; if I ate injection-filled tofu all the time, it'd probably be just fine. I tried to hide the flavor by covering the block of tofu (minus one bite) with a liberal helping of shaved bonito, then brought it out to Satoe.

"Hey, want some tofu? It's injection-filled, I bought it special. I made yakko-dofu."

Sure, Satoe said. I passed her the dish and some chopsticks, and she started to eat.

"How is it? Rather tasty, wouldn't you agree?"

"Mm-hmm. Mm-hmm."

Satoe was bent over the plate, eating the injection-filled tofu. A wife bent over, eating. A totally ordinary, everyday sight, but for the past few days things had been peculiar inside the house, the space itself flickering, holes appearing here and there, stuffed with straw or thick rope to plug them up. Reality's growing thin, the telephone and radio signals aren't coming through properly. I'd be thinking, when suddenly a record would start to play. It seemed to me that the house itself must've been injection-filled with some kind of peculiar air. And that woman who showed up at our front door last week must've been the one who did the injecting.

I knew she was crazy the second I saw her. First off, her outfit was totally outlandish. I don't know how old she was, but she was clearly too old to be wearing a micro mini skirt like that, with flower pattern fishnets to boot, a light, salmon-colored sweater under a black cardigan that might've been fashionable right after the war, and a hopelessly outmoded silver brooch with some shitty cloisonné pinned at her solar plexus. She had a face like the Utz girl past her prime, but it was her eyes that were really disconcerting: she had eyes like a drainage ditch choked with algae. Eutrophic from an overabundance of nutrients. Nutrient-rich eyes. The very thought repulsed me.

"There must be some mistake," I said, but her eutrophic eyes snapped wide open and she just stood there in silence, staring me dead in the face, and just when it was starting to get to me, she repeated herself: "But I, I saw it. Your performance," so what could I do, I repeated myself too.

"I've never performed anything in my life."

"Of course you have. I mean, I saw you. With my own eyes."

"What exactly was it you saw?"

"You were singing, with a look in your eyes like a sick dog. Everyone was booing, but you just kept singing away with this anguished look on your face. And some guy ran up on stage and smashed your guitar..."

"I keep telling you! I don't know anything about any performance." She was so stubborn that I finally lost it and started shouting. But she didn't even flinch, she just stared into my face with those unsettling nutrient-rich eyes of hers. I started to feel like I was the one who was wrong here, and I looked away. At which she started in again with some confounding nonsense. "I got really hung up on your level of consciousness and I couldn't let it go, I just had to ask you about it, so at last I bit the bullet and here I am."

Once she finally went home, I noticed something unfamiliar lying on the tiled floor of the entryway; I picked it up, and it was one of those little fish-shaped plastic soy sauce bottles you sometimes get with takeout, but instead of soy sauce, this one was filled with a strange white fluid. And the bummer was that the little red cap wasn't on properly, so when I picked it up, the white fluid leaked out all over my hand and gave off a smell like the rotting entrails of an animal, it made my fingers all sticky so I hurried to wash them off but they stunk forevermore, and before long the holes started opening up in space and the phone flipped horizontally and whatnot. Shit. What had that fucking woman injected into my house? Shit. Yoshihara's making it, he's married to a knockout like Tomiko, he's appearing on *Now, Villager*, even, and what the fuck am I doing? Eating injection-filled tofu in a house full of holes and letting some crazy lady railroad me like that. Thinking of Tomiko only redoubled my agony. Dammit, what the hell was I thinking, I had that marriage handed to me on a silver platter and I blew it, slurping that eel and everything, then I married Satoe but now I'm head over heels for Tomiko. Rapid flows the stream/The torrent once riven in twain/By the damming rock/Shall surely someday meet again/To flow as one once more—Retired Emperor Sutoku. It's unbearably heartrending so I do my best not to, but I end up thinking about Tomiko like this four or five times a day—her expressions, her gestures, her kimono, her figure and all the rest float into my mind, and when they do, I'm made keenly aware of the fact that my precious Tomiko is the wife of a worthless worm like Yoshihara and my heart is smashed to pieces, I'm climbing the walls, crawling out of my skin.

In a reverie, I daydreamed of winning Tomiko's love. First I start to paint again like I used to. And I win the Gölmar prize, just like Yoshihara, then I'm the one in the limelight, all eyes on me. Yoshihara's stock plummets in inverse proportion, his talent and finances both going down the drain. I send Yoshihara an invitation to my solo show. Droves of people show up to the opening. Newspaper reporters with shoulder bags arrive to interview me. "It seems to me a certain...rebellious spirit, I guess you'd say, runs consistently through all of your work. How does that strike you?"

"Hmm, I suppose I do have a rebellious spirit. That sort of thing is at the root of—"

"Hey, congratulations!" Kizaki comes over and cuts in.

"Hey, thanks. You get yourself a drink?"

"Yeah, but this wine's garbage."

"Oh yeah?"

"Yeah. It's garbage. Just like your paintings."

"Maybe so. But remember this: you fuckers

are gonna be drinking garbage wine for the rest of your miserable little lives. With the money I make from my garbage paintings, I'll be enjoying the good stuff. You got that? Do you? Then get out of my sight. Fucking asshole." Uncle Kudai, my sister and her husband, my friends from school, Kitada's mother, they're all there too. And some of our business connections. And some government bureaucrats. And Inō. And Boss Baldy and his cronies. The dazzling master holding court, surrounded by reporters and fans. Some burly cretins I've never seen before are bustling around keeping a watchful eye on the proceedings. The ox-headed singer provides the entertainment.

A man and woman lean inconspicuously against the wall in a corner. The woman, wearing Western clothes unlike the previous year, is violently beautiful, isn't she, in an out-of-tune kind of way; ground down by daily life, her careworn fatigue muddies her beauty, static in the signal. The man, on the other hand, is a titchy little fellow with a mass of disheveled hair, almond eyes, and a narrow nose, dressed up in the same turmeric-colored suit he'd worn last year; in better times he might've come off as a young gentleman, but brought low like this he presents as a seedy low-life, maybe a petty bureaucrat. One of life's little mysteries.

"Hey, how come you're not eating? No need to hold back. Eat up!"

"Thanks, I...don't have much of an appetite. I'll just have a little champagne."

"Champagne, right, let's see. Doesn't look like there's any champagne. There's beer and wine, though."

"I'll pass."

"Come on, don't be like that. It'll save us the cost of a meal. There's nothing to eat at home. Can't pass up an opportunity like this. Look, they have chicken, they have beans. There's a sushi station over there, hell, they even have cake! Oh."

"Oh."

"Oh."

"Hey."

"..."

"Hey." I grin. Yoshihara can't look me in

the eye. Damn right. I'm shining with an overpowering luster. Blustery shine. Lustrous beast. Yoshihara, by contrast, is skin and bones, and the instant he sees me, he starts trembling and stammering incomprehensible nonsense under his breath. "Ah. Please excuse me. Please, wait a moment. Yes. Sorry to make you wait. Excuse me. Yesss. Sorry to have kept you waiting." In a disgustingly classy tone, I ask them, "Can I get you anything?" but Yoshihara just keeps on like before. "Ah, you'll really have to excuse me. Yesss, please wait a moh woh woh. Yesss. Excuse me." Total communication breakdown. He's completely cracked. Ignoring Yoshihara and his constant stream of Please excuse us, moh woh woh, "Haven't seen you since the observation tower. How've you been?" I say to Tomiko, fixing her with the rakish gaze of an old Hollywood scoundrel. Tomiko returns my gaze with nutrient-rich eyes. My composure melts away and I blurt out, "Oh, please excuse me. I'll bring you some champagne, so woh woh woh, I'll fetch it straight away, please excuse me, moh woh."

"What'd you say?" asked Satoe suspiciously.

"I didn't say anything."

"You were grinning and saying moh woh woh or something."

"Oh, that. That was nothing, I was just doing an impression of this old guy from the parking garage in Namikichō," I said on my way out of the living room.

I'd only taken a few steps before my face got jammed into a hole. It stank of straw. And dust. Stifling.

Isn't the morning sunlight beautiful... If the light were like this all day long, the tears in space might even close up, but around eleven the air slowly starts getting filthier and the light turns back into regular old pedestrian light. Sad. But at least it's beautiful right now. The sickle protruding from the tatami glittering in the slanting sunlight. I traced the outline of the sickle on the canvas. I painted the weave of the tatami, I painted the torn paper of the sliding door, I painted the light that was injecting the air with energy, I painted the shadows... Lastly I added in a bamboo motif. But the only thing on the canvas was an inexplicable mass of squiggles squiggling around, for which I had no explanation. Desperate now, I tried adding the Marunouchi Building and some monkeys. But even those were unrecognizable. Which isn't because I'm bad at painting, mind you, it's just that I've only got one color of paint, I mean, shit, once I'd laid down 800 yen for the canvas, 3,000 for the brush, and 2,000 for a tube of oil paint, there was only a grand left over, but that's where skill and ingenuity come in. I figured I could cope with the situation by applying the paint thinly in some places, thickly in others, really heaping it up when I had to, but once I was done, all I was left with was a bunch of scarlet squiggles. I threw the brush at the wall and flung myself down on the bed. I could hear a *plink plink plink* coming from the company housing next door, the daughter of an engineer for some brewery practicing the piano.

Light glinted off the tempered part of the sickle, the part that looks kind of like a mackerel—the "blade pattern," I think they call it?—and even the normally unbearable tatami, with its scuffs and scars and general discoloration, appeared in this light as if it had been caressed with a holy brush, coated with a scintillating power, every detail standing out in stark relief down to the individual stitches in the weave. So it was with the sliding door, and so it was with the empty teacup that had rolled beside the sickle. It was as if all the normally oppressive pieces of life were purified by the light, which was the whole reason I wanted to paint it all in the first place.

And now this. If I just had more paints, I muttered, picking up the brush, and in between the Marunouchi Building and the monkeys I wrote Paints. Money. Bread. Nope, still unrecognizable. As the sun rose higher, I watched the area around the sickle sink quickly into gloom.

Uncle Kudai had really pulled our fat out of the fire. My sister and I were on track to end up saddled with massive debt after our mom died, but the crafty old bastard worked his magic and made all our liabilities disappear. And our inheritance right along with them. Everyone said that, all in all, it was cause for celebration. Glad to hear it, thanks for letting me know. But, here's the thing. If some loan shark had been telling me

Pay up, asshole, I'll kill you, I'll bury you, and I went to Uncle Kudai and said Please help me, please do something, and he somehow got rid of my debts, it's not like I wouldn't be grateful, I'd think, That was a close one, you really saved my ass, but that's not what happened, he said, Your debts are gone. And so is your inheritance, which didn't exactly fill me with gratitude, that is, even if I wouldn't go so far as to say Uncle Kudai had done something illicit to help us out, I mean, shouldn't we at least have ended up with the house? Did Uncle Kudai misappropriate it? I can't deny that these doubts and suspicions might have crossed my mind, which is to say, they did. But that was clearly just the warped jealousy of poverty speaking, these unseemly thoughts bubbling up simply because I was now broke, which is exactly why I had to hurry up and finish this painting so I could win the Gölmar Prize, for which I needed to buy paints, but where was I going to get the money? That was easy: I'd borrow it. I'd been figuring on that for a while now anyway. But I wouldn't be incurring this debt because I'd frittered away my money on debauched pleasures and could no longer make ends meet, no, this was an investment in my new career as a painter, plus, we're only talking about a few hundred thousand yen here, and let's get real, anyone who couldn't finagle that much from his friends at this age was obviously a moron. A bit of bone from the old bag. White with ash. A hazy pelvis.

Unlike some shitheaded sons of bitches I know, I've got plenty of friends. There are always throngs of insincere, superficial people surrounding Yoshihara at his parties and his exhibitions, but let's be honest, it's all a bit like "Toshishun"—when things are going well it's all very well, but when push comes to shove they're nowhere to be seen. They're all totally superficial and shallow, and I think it's safe to say they don't have a single brain cell between them. Take the other day, for example. I went to the opening of Yoshihara's new exhibition out of a desire to see Tomiko again, knowing full well that I'd be totally out of my element as always, and there was this guy there, I don't know how the hell they knew each other, although, Yoshihara's a celebrity now so I guess he associates with people like that, but anyway, there was this giant of a man in traditional clothes with his hair done up in a topknot that has no place in this day and age—a top-division sumo wrestler whose ring name was Kudoyama or something like that. This Kudoyama looked like he lived his life completely isolated from the outside world. He was flanked by two miniaturized versions of himself, like the stone dogs outside a shrine, and he appeared totally satisfied in his own little universe, remaining expressionless as if he didn't even notice everyone pointing and whispering because to the outside observer his outlandish physique seemed like something out of a fairy tale, but you had to wonder if it wasn't the society of dwarfs constantly swarming around his feet that seemed like fiction in Kudoyama's eyes.

All the fashionable and fictionable people had their own take on Kudoyama, but their opinions didn't amount to shit, it was all just, "Wowww," "He's the real deal," "He's ginormous," "He's the real deal," "He could crush me with one punch," "He's the real deal," but one woman in a yellow suit really took the cake. I guess when she saw him, she just couldn't hold it in: "He's sooo fat."

'Course he fuckin' is! Or should I say, Of course he fucking is! But the woman just said exactly what had popped into her artless little head, and all the media-type goons surrounding her just responded with superficial, perfunctory agreement: "He sure is fat! Sooo, sooo fat!"

Doesn't bode well for Yoshihara's future, spending his life surrounded by all these superficial, shallow people who can only engage with the world according to their moment-to-moment perceptions of it. I, on the other hand, am blessed with more contemplative friends. Now if I can only get one of them to lend me the money for some paints, it'll be a cinch to show Yoshihara up. And when I do, there's Tomiko. OK, off to Kizaki's. I threw down the brush and started groping around in the bamboo letter rack on the wall.

It was the first time I'd ever been to Kizaki's place. We always met at art galleries or fancy parfait shops, which had nothing to do with the fact that we'd gotten older; come to think of it, even when we were kids I'd never once been to his house. Happenstance?

In the righthand slot, written in angular characters: KNOW YOU ON THIS FIRST DAY OF THE NEW YEAR THAT SUNDRY NATIONS BELGIË ROSSIYA ALL SHALL PERISH BURNT TO ASH HAPPY NEW YEAR; in the middle one, a picture of a slave holding a gigantic musical instrument and singing; and in the lefthand slot, to match the one on the right, a card from Kizaki with Don't you know how this year is going to go? How's your mom shall perish the thought hahaha scrawled on it, which, despite being from this past New Year's, was faded and yellowed as if it had been sent decades ago, and on it Kizaki's address: Yashiho 1244. A part of town I'd never seen. Scene.

A station on a slope. Fallow fields and a sloping stone wall and scattered wooden houses. I exited the unmanned station, like a concrete cube that had just been deposited there and then forgotten, and climbed the nominally paved road that wound up the grade, zigzagging back and forth between the stone wall on the left and the grassy slope on the right, headed Kizaki-ward. The sun high overhead. My shadow, rich and black.

"I feel kind of depressed," said Kizaki, kicking the woman's head that lay fallen at his feet. The disembodied head flew across the room and bounced off the woman's torso that hung pale in the darkness of the sitting room beyond.

"Should you be doing that?"

"Why not? I'm depressed," answered Kizaki in a brighter tone, some small sense of catharsis coloring his voice.

"Yeah, but aren't you trying to sell those? You're being kind of rough with them..."

"It's fine. The company went under."

"What? Went under?"

"Yup."

"Then, what about your guarantee?"

"Gone."

"That's awful."

"Nah, it's fine, but I'm sick of looking at these chicks. It's making me depressed," Kizaki replied, surveying the army of finished products in the sitting room and the heap of heads and arms in the living room, not to mention the mannequins stacked in the entryway that hadn't even made it out of the packaging. I picked up a head that lay at my feet. The half-finished woman only had one eye. A smooth half-visage. Face. Gently I returned it to the floor.

"So, what's up?" he asked. "Remind me why you came out here?"

I got right to the point. "I was wondering if you could lend me some money. I think I said as much on the phone, but..."

"'Fraid not," Kizaki came back immediately.

"Yeah, I figured," and just like that, my fundraising hopes fizzled.

Kizaki and I stood there in silence. Flies clustered restlessly on the woman's head by my feet.

"But since you came all this way, have something to eat before you go. I'm too depressed so I was just about to prepare my luncheon anyway," said Kizaki, walking off down the hallway to the left. I followed without a word.

The ramshackle DIY kitchen addition he had constructed out of two-by-fours and corrugated metal was warped and peppered with gaps, and over time mud and leaves had found their way in and plastered themselves to every surface. There was a gold-colored pot resting on a burner that was hooked up to a propane tank by a rubber hose, and Kizaki scooped something out of it with a bowl then handed it to me. I couldn't place the flavor, so I asked What is this? to which he replied simply, Gruel, and with a look of stoic endurance he started shoveling the enigmatic meal down his gullet with a pair of chopsticks. The kitchen was teeming with flies. There were meat and vegetable scraps strewn everywhere, along with more arms and half-faces. It was the definition of disarray. I remembered that Kizaki was married, and asked, "Oh yeah, how's your wife?" Kizaki didn't reply, then after a while said seemingly to himself, "I'm depressed," then more clearly, "You done?" tossing both our bowls into the sink and emptying the pot into the bushes before tossing it into the sink as well. Explained why there were so many flies.

"See ya."

"See ya."

"I'll call you soon."

"See ya."

Kizaki had made it abundantly clear that he was depressed. Abundant as the thick grass growing all around his house. He was blue. Bluegrass. Verdant weeds as far as the eye could see. When I got back to the road that led to the station, the flies formed a thick mass right in front of my face, blocking my path. I couldn't deal with the thought of cutting through the swarm, so I hurled a rock, but the flies didn't budge. There was a flat arc of undergrowth to the left of the road, and I had no choice but to go that way to avoid them. On my way I happened on a corrugated metal shed about the size of a telephone booth, a discarded red women's sandal lying in the doorway. An acrid stench wafted from it and it seemed to be the source of the flies, who were apparently pissed that I had passed that way because they started going berserk, ramming into my eyes and hair and chest and arms, filthy and foul; clutching my head and squeezing my eyes shut I broke through the maelstrom of flies, the maelstrom of filth, and made it back to the road. A dwindling retinue of flies pursued me all the way back to the station. Don't get too attached to me, flies. Don't expect anything from me.

Squatting on the concrete platform, I watched a faded burgundy train lumber up the slope with a dopey rattle. Its languid approach made me happy for some reason, and I sprung lightly aboard, but the scent of humiliation that had entered my nostrils and saturated my brain wasn't going away. Evening before I knew it.

Seated at a low table heaped with all kinds of stuffed pastries cut in half, the yakisoba and croquettes sandwiched inside spilling out, Sarubashi Umasute was just about to dig in. Care to join me? he asked, smiling graciously.

"Man, you're really going for it. Nothing but baked goods, same as always."

"It's all just unsold stock," Sarubashi replied brightly, picking one up.

"What kind is that?"

"This one's, um...I forget."

"'I forget'? What do you mean, 'I forget,' you made it yourself!"

"Well, yeah, but sales have plummeted lately 'cause nothin' tastes good, so I've been trying out all kinds of new products."

"That bad, huh?"

"Yup. Only took in three hundred yen today."

"Damn."

Another fool's errand. I figured since the bakery was a cash business Sarubashi would have some money on hand to lend me, so I'd come even though it was already past dark, but all for naught. I immediately started looking for a chance to make my exit. A weird odor drifted out of the dark interior of the shop.

"But, still. How do you come up with new recipes?"

"Ah, well, that's the rub. I mean, look, I just make the dough, it was my wife who made the filling. But the thing is, she split recently."

Sarubashi's wife? I couldn't conjure an image of her. No recollection whatsoever. Which is neither here nor there, but I could feel the conversation heading in a dangerous direction. "You don't say," I answered, not actually caring in the slightest, and definitely not caring if he knew it, which is to say making that fact pretty clear, but

Sarubashi just plowed ahead.

"See, my wife..."

"What about her?"

"She got obsessed with feng shui."

"Feng shui."

"Uh huh."

"That doesn't sound so bad."

"It is that bad."

"What is?"

"The feng shui, for cryin' out loud. Feng shui. Ever heard of it? Feng shui?"

"Yeah, I've heard of feng shui. Like, put yellow flowers in this direction or whatever, right?"

"That's the one, yeah. But my wife got into a heavier version of it, or maybe she was doing it wrong or something, but it...wasn't normal."

"What do you mean, 'wasn't normal'?"

"The whole thing was batshit. She stuck a hatchet in the tabletop, hung a pickling stone from the lintel with a piece of rope..."

"Weird, my wife stuck a sickle in the tatami... Wonder if that was the same shit."

"No question. Didn't they read the same book about it?"

"Did they?"

"Yeah. And I didn't have a clue what was going on at first, so I figured it was an accident and pulled the hatchet out of the table. Which turned into a whole thing, and I said, Feng shui's fine, but how 'bout you stick to the nice, quiet kind. Then my wife said, All the nice, quiet feng shui in the world can't help this shithole of a bakery. Can you fucking believe that? I couldn't stand hearing her badmouth the bakery that way, so I took the hatchet to her head."

"What??"

"Well, the handle."

"I would hope so."

"Obviously. And I held back, I mean, I did it so it wouldn't hurt, but my wife being the way she is, she completely lost it, went totally berserk. And when women get like that, forget about holding back, they don't know the meaning of the word, know what I mean?"

"Totally."

"She starts throwing everything she can get her hands on, and finally ends up waving the hatchet around, right."

"Uh huh."

"And I thought she was gonna kill me, so I ran out of the house. Went to the izakaya, had a few drinks, and when I got back, the place was trashed and my wife was nowhere to be seen."

"And that was it? She never came back?"

"Nope."

"That's rough."

"Not really, except that I don't know how to make the fillings. I had no choice but to make 'em myself, but they turned out awful, and see, the only people we get coming in here are the folks from the neighborhood. Just regulars who come every day. So they notice if anything tastes even a tiny bit different. Sales have dropped off a cliff. So I've been trying to restore our good name by putting new things on the menu."

Sarubashi's gaze fell to the mountain of pastries in front of him. Seemed like he was having a rough time of it. But I was having a rough time, too. I couldn't handle talking about baked goods any longer, so I said something meaningless like, Well, you know, that's how things go, I guess, and started to get up. "Oh. Heading home?" Sarubashi asked bluntly, without a shred of tact, which absolved me of any similar obligation, so I just stood up and said, "Yup. I was hoping to borrow that money from you, but if that's how things are, guess I'd better just head home." Sarubashi stared up at me from where he sat. There was something crepuscular in the bright white fluorescent light that illuminated his face from above. Dark shadows pooled beneath his eyes and nose, rendering Sarubashi's seemingly carefree face corpselike.

"I hate to ask," he said, reaching out and picking up one of the pastries from the table, "but before you go, can you try this and tell me what you think? I've been sampling so many that I can't tell what's what anymore." It was a round bun, not stuffed with anything. When I tore off a piece, the dough was a light greenish color and there were flecks of something that looked like white cheese mixed in.

It existed in a dimension entirely separate from any concept of good or bad. I had eaten Sarubashi's baking before, and there'd always been something distinctive about the dough—

old-fashioned pastries that went perfectly with the simple fillings, the kind of thing you get an uncontrollable hankering for sometimes. This bun, on the other hand, tasted like toxic waste. The most unsettling part, though, was the bristles that seemed to be mixed into the dough, like something from an old brush, truly unpleasant to have inside one's mouth, and when I tried to gulp the thing down as fast as possible, they stuck in all over my mouth and got caught, I couldn't manage to get any of it down my gullet, Han oo hive he so' hawter. Hawter, hawter, I said to Sarubashi, and once he got me some water I finally managed to choke it all down. Sarubashi asked anxiously, "W-What do you think?" and I gave it to him straight: It's like eating an old brush mixed into toxic waste. "That's what I was afraid of," Sarubashi responded dismally. "A customer came into the shop today ranting and raving at me."

"Sounds about right."

"I knew I couldn't make a proper filling, so I tried kneading different meat extracts and whatnot into the dough itself... No good though, huh?

Guess the shaver didn't do anybody any favors, either."

"The shaver?" I asked, suddenly concerned.

"Uh huh, regular meat's too expensive." Well that really clears things up. "If you need to borrow money, try Yoshihara. He's on TV all the time these days, he's probably rolling in it. I can't fucking stand it. And his wife's such a babe." The words issued from his cadaverous face. My own face went cold, my mind and heart exploded. I still had brushmouth. I left Sarubashi Umasute's house. On my way out, I passed the kitchen. It reeked, like someone had spilled acetic acid everywhere.

The last bus dropped me off, and after it drove away it was pitch dark. The area was overgrown, thick grass blanketing the raised plot that was like a farmer's field that was like a vacant lot behind the bus stop, not to mention the empty lot in front of the shabby, one-story agricultural co-op building, surrounded by a low concrete wall. Come to think of it, the grass around Kizaki's place had been pretty overgrown this afternoon, too, but the vibe was totally different.

The grass around Kizaki's house had been a bright, grassy green that gave a ferocious impression of abundant liveliness, vitality, vigor; this grass, by contrast, was a deep, gloomy green, tall, glistening with an oily sheen, growing there as if by some sinister design. Maybe it was just that it was night? Gah! I reached out to pluck a blade of grass and cut myself on it. Crossing the road, I held up my finger in the ring of illumination from a slender streetlight in front of what might have been a credit union, a moth the size of a sparrow battering itself against the bulb. I couldn't believe how deep the cut was. It was gushing blood. That grass was like a sickle. Sickle grass. Brigadier General Sicklegrass. I need the mindset of a general if I'm going to do this. This cut on my finger would be a trifle to a general. I put my finger in my mouth. The tang of salt. I took it back out and wiped it on my pants, then put it in my mouth again as I started down the narrow path between the credit union and a parking lot.

I no longer harbored any doubt. I knew what I had to do. In the Mountain Dew-green light of the bus, I had made up my mind, to wit: It would definitely be humiliating to ask Yoshihara for a loan. But Kizaki and Sarubashi Umasute were both in dire straits, and Yoshihara was the only other person who might even plausibly lend me money. Ergo, I would borrow money from Yoshihara, it was as simple as that. As to the manner in which I would endure this humiliation, that was simple too: I would ask him for a loan with a servile smile plastered on my face, bowing and scraping like I was *wretched*, and *impoverished*, all the while addressing him as "Sir" and so forth. Yoshihara's always been a real piece of shit, so when his old friend shows up in straitened circumstances, he'll act like he's better than me even though we're the same fucking age, prancing around like some aristocrat in his fancy kimono and his navy blue tabi, "Mmhmmhmm, ohoho, hehehe, so you've got no money. I always knew you were no good, and it looks like I was right. So now you've come begging for money like some little urchin, eh?"

"Have you taken a look around at our country lately? This great nation is in crisis, we've got no room for idlers like you. So how about this? I'll write you a letter of introduction, and you can set about finding your fortune overseas. How does that strike you?"

"Hm? The work? It will be noble work indeed. I'm talking about building schools and digging wells for people in the developing world. And, clearing landmines. Wouldn't that be much more worthwhile than frittering away your time as you've been doing here?" But he has no intention of writing me a letter of introduction, he's just saying these things to humiliate me. He really is a piece of shit, through and through. "I'm sorry to say I can't do that. I have my wife to think about it," I say, sounding like some kind of serf. At which Yoshihara puts on an exaggerated show of saying, "Ah yes, that's right. You got married. I had completely forgotten. Yes, of course," then continues with a contrived nod. "Right. Well, here's what we'll do. Let's forget about a loan. Because, let's be honest, you'd never pay it back anyway. Agreed? But please don't misunderstand, it's not that I'm some kind of miser. No, I'm saying this because it would be bad for *you* if I lent you the money. If I gave you a loan, it would be the same as giving you a handout. And as a friend, I have no desire to see you reduced to begging for alms. So what I'm going to do," Yoshihara begins, slipping a coin purse out of the breast of his kimono and flipping through some bills with a hairy finger. On it his platinum wedding band. "What I'm going to do, my friend, is not lend you this money, but give it to you. And I'm not just giving it to you, I'm giving it to you as a wedding present. As I'm constantly telling my wife, for a man like you to marry an illiterate hostess only magnifies your collective misfortune, hahaha. But that's neither here nor there. Now," he says, holding out the money, "please accept this token of my congratulations." Bowing, I take it from him. The end. Everything's going swimmingly. The first stage of my plan is complete. In other words, don't count me out yet, Yoshihara. I hold the rank of brigadier general. You've got the makings of a sergeant major at best, so you're oblivious to my tactics and stratagems, standing there with your head up your ass, so pleased with yourself in your kimono like you're some kind of aristocrat, walking all over your old acquaintance, hahaha. What a fool. The only reason I adopted that servile attitude was to put you off your guard. Ever read *The Thirty-Six Stratagems*? I very much doubt it. But you just saw one of them in action. And you fell for it, hook, line and sinker. Wahaha. You have no idea what this money is for. Hahaha. Thanks to this money, I'm going to outstrip you, surpass you, hahaha. Go ahead and cry. With the paints I buy using the money *you* gave me, I'll complete my masterpiece, and your days at the top will be numbered. And then that trophy wife of yours will abandon you like the calculating woman she always was. Wahaha. And I think we both know who she'll run to then. Do you see this? Behold my malice. Sicklegrass's glistening revenge. The ingenuity of General Sicklegrass spells the end for Yoshihara. My rank is brigadier general. My mind is titanium. Thoroughly resolved now, I sniveled down a path flanked on either side by stakes wrapped in annealed wire. A path between stands of tall grass. A dark, narrow path made somehow more forlorn by the feeble yellow light. My finger was split open.

I moved the paintbrush across the canvas to the strains of a solo piano, eating ham and drinking whiskey. Which may sound elegant, but in fact it was anything but, which is to say that each aspect was a humiliation in its own right, each brushstroke filling me with frustrated impatience. Blue sky, I thought, gazing out the window at the blue sky, then turned my attention back to painting the sickle spinning through the sky of the canvas, my frustration mounting.

The piano, for its part, wasn't elegant because it was a six-year-old girl playing it. She had started practicing just as I began work on the sickle, playing the same faltering notes over and over and over again, which would've been bad enough if the song itself hadn't been some practice piece with nothing whatsoever to recommend it. While I didn't make a lick of progress on my painting, though, her playing slowly but surely started to sound like music. Preshazonnn! Aha. I'll add another sickle. Something silver was proceeding slowly across the blue sky. Must be an airplane. Gotta be. That said, here's the thing about dashing off an airplane: I've tried to paint them a million times but they always come out totally wrong, so I don't even try anymore. Because I'm a pro. For what it's worth. Because I'm no amateur. The weave of the tatami molders on.

Though that said, the real problem here is this ham. I received the ham amid a flash of light.

This flash of light enveloped me as I stood in the doorway of Mr. and Mrs. Yoshihara's home, which was even more lavish than I expected, or could even have imagined. Tomiko answered the door and, what was it she said, oh yeah, she said, Wait a moment. I'll go ask him. Felt like just a whiff, just a presence. She returned right away and asked, What's it about? I hesitated. I mean, of course I did. Telling the object of your secret desire that I was hoping, if I might, to be allowed to entreat your successful husband to lend me some money isn't exactly smooth. Corpuscles of larval light worm their way into the blue of the sky. But my mind is titanium. I am Brigadier General Sicklegrass. I spoke with the intrepid spirit granted me by heaven. But, I made a backroom deal with myself. A small deal, but a deal nonetheless: To act every inch the old school chum. Like they did it in the old days. You know, rough and tumble. Casual, informal, no need to hold back, as if me and Yoshihara had been like family back when we were students.

"I wanna borrow some cash. Nothing major, ten grand or so'd be plenty. Man, back in school that woulda been a fortune. We were lucky if we could scrape together three grand for yakitori, and I'm pretty sure I was the one who always paid."

"You don't say." Tomiko took in my appearance with a supercilious eye. How did I look to her? The texture of old brush in my mouth, on my tongue. Blood oozing from my finger. I wiped it on the ass of my pants.

No point in turning on the lights for someone looking for a handout. I stood waiting in the gloom of the entryway. The faint glow of the lamp by the front gate filtering in through the stained glass on either side of the door provided the only illumination. Tomiko returned with a handful of cash, not even bothering to put it in an envelope, and passed it to me. "He told me to give you his best," she said, looking me over once again with that look of haughty appraisal. Titanium mind. "Tell him I said thanks," I replied, matching the rhythm of my words to hers. As I laid my hand on the doorknob to leave, Tomiko added, "Oh, that's right. He also said to take that ham while you're at it," pointing to a pile of gifts heaped up in the corner of the entryway. An extravagant ring locked and loaded around her finger. In that moment I thought: You think you're better than me? Sure, maybe I needed to borrow some money. But that was a legitimate loan, I haven't fallen so low that you can pawn your gift ham off on me. What am I, some decrepit old fart? You think I'll eat what you fuckers won't? Get off your high horse. But, I only thought those things, and in reality I said something else entirely. Something like, "Ahaha. Looks delicious. That ham really does look delicious. Hah, I sure do love ham. Thanks a million, Missus. What a treat. I'm much obliged, I sure am," putting on a performance that was far more servile and excessively emotive than it needed to be, telling myself all the while that the only reason I could manage the mental acrobatics of such reverse psychology was thanks to my titanium mind.

But Tomiko, whose beauty was her only asset and who never ventured to peer into the abyss of human life, could never understand such things. She stepped all the way down into the entryway now, saying, This is just taking up space, and we don't need this either, sorting through the gifts and pulling out a bottle of wine and some more ham, but as she labored thus she leaned in over the pile of gifts so that her chest and mini-skirted thighs were exposed, her figure suddenly entrancing and aphrodisiacal in the extreme. Clouds gathered in my mind and heart. My muscles twitched, and just as I reached out to touch her shoulder, the entryway was flooded with blinding light. A flash of blinding light in the entryway. Blood still oozing from my finger.

A shrill laugh resounded from the doorway. "Excellent. Excellent. Excellent." Yoshihara was standing there with a camera, a thick padded kimono slung around the shoulders of his yukata. He looked drunk, his face a deep red as if someone had upturned an entire vat of sappanwood dye over his head, and he continued absurdly repeating Excellent as he snapped away with his camera, not caring that the hem of his yukata was in disarray, and after a while he looked down like he was making sure of something, grumbling to himself and fiddling with a round knob-ish thing on top of the camera, until finally he said, There we go. Okay. Tomiko, come over here a sec, glancing at me and then whispering something in her ear. They both looked at me, then, and laughed in unison before disappearing into the depths of the house, all tangled up with one another. For my part, I departed ham in hand. A yellow afterimage. Titanium or no.

I'll paint it. That afterimage, on the blue sky. Along with Yoshihara's flippant yet demoniac eyes. And you know what, I do want to paint an airplane after all. Though I'm worried the airplane might throw off the overall balance. You know what, I'd better do a dry run, a preliminary sketch, that kind of thing. I'll practice on the ham.

First I tried painting Yoshihara's eyes on the thick-cut ham. Feels good. Mmm. Uh huh. Now if only I can recreate the way this feeling feels on the canvas. But, it probably only feels this way because of the meaty texture of the ham, huh. Do I slap the ham on the canvas? It needs a narrative, sure, but the blue sky is the most important thing, it's that blue sky I want to feel. With the day's dust and the day's warmth still permeating the weave of the tatami, Ooh. I'll blue-skyify it. Ham eyes in the blue sky. And the airplane moving through it all. Tearing open the sky. The silver airplane. Abstract silver. But the wicked ham eyes are glittering. Okay, this is where I really need to put myself out there. I doffed the 10,000-franc wool coat and stood naked to the waist. Squatting in a low, wide stance, I spread my hands like a sumo wrestler preparing for a match and dominated the sky with my eyes popped open as wide as they would go. And not just one of me. Like the multitudes of buddhas and bodhisattvas positioned around a mandala, a horde of mes both large and small arced through the blue sky, trembling lightly as they bobbed in the air, eyes bulging. The silver airplane wends its way through the intervals and interstices between, but finds its way blocked by the ham eyes, eyes on the cut face of the rosy meat, marbled with white fat. Dark, nutrient-rich eyes. Flitting about in uncountable numbers, and why the hell they would do this I have no idea, maybe they were jealous, they began harassing the airplane, sticking to the fuselage and smearing slime and shame in equal measure, or plastering themselves against the windshield and making it impossible to see. The airplane lost its equilibrium, and after wobbling through the sky a little longer it finally fell into a tailspin, smashing into the ground and exploding in a column of flame, black smoke rising to the sky along with a heinous odor that reached all the way up here. There was nothing I could do, I simply watched the whole thing unfold with eyes a-bulge. Reigning o'er the sky as I was, though, it was too shameful to just stand by and watch, so the mandala of roughly forty mes of all sizes formed a perfect circle and, eyes wide, began revolving like a Ferris wheel and reciting the Diamond Sutra on behalf of the airplane. Black smoke rising from the ground. The sickle glinting in the tatami.

Enough already, thought one of me. But the me who thought this was a relatively small one, as it happened, and as long as the larger ones didn't think so, we'd all continue wheeling through the sky and chanting the sutra: I SHALL LEAD ALL SENTIENT BEINGS TO NIRVANA, BE THEY BORN OF EGG OR BORN OF WOMB, BORN OF MOISTURE OR BORN MIRACULOUSLY OF THEMSELVES, THOSE WITH FORM AND THOSE WITHOUT, THOSE WITH PERCEPTION AND THOSE WITHOUT, THOSE WITH NO-PERCEPTION AND THOSE WITHOUT. THERE ALL SHALL MEET WITH THE EXTINCTION OF SUFFERING. AND THE SENTIENT BEINGS THUS LIBERATED SHALL BE IMMEASURABLE, INNUMERABLE, LIMITLESS. My selves kept on turning.

Enough already, thought another one of me. But the wheel didn't stop spinning; if anything, it started moving faster, and I began to feel dizzy. And what's more, the me who had thought it this time wasn't a small one like before, he was on the larger side of average, so he should've had some say in the matter, but still the wheel didn't stop turning. What the hell's going on here, my head is swimming. I'm sweating, I feel nauseous. Stop spinning! Stop chanting! If it keeps on like this I'm gonna die, thought almost all of me, but still the spinning wouldn't stop, THUS I SAY, DWELL NOT ON FORM IN CHARITY. DWELL NOT ON SOUND OR SMELL OR TASTE OR TOUCH WHEN PRACTICING CHARITY, SUBHŪTI. A BODHISATTVA SHOULD THUS NOT DWELL ON ANY ATTRIBUTE WHEN PRACTICING CHARITY. WHY? IF THE BODHISATTVA DWELLS NOT ON ANY ATTRIBUTE WHEN PRACTICING CHARITY, THE MERIT PRODUCED SHALL BE BEYOND COMPREHENSION. WHAT DO YOU THINK, SUBHŪTI, IS THE SPACE TO THE EAST MEASURABLE? NO, WORLD-HONORED ONE. WHAT THEN, SUBHŪTI, OF THE SPACE TO THE SOUTH, THE WEST, THE NORTH, THE FOUR INTERMEDIATE DIRECTIONS, ABOVE AND BELOW? ARE THESE MEASURABLE? NO, WORLD-HONORED ONE. AND SO IS IT WITH THE MERIT PRODUCED BY THE BODHISATTVA WHO PRACTICES CHARITY WITHOUT DWELLING ON ANY ATTRIBUTE, SUBHŪTI. THIS TOO IS IMMEASURABLE. SUBHŪTI, IT IS UPON THIS

TEACHING ALONE THAT THE BODHISATTVA SHOULD DWELL. Teeheehee, one of the especially big mes cackled in delight as we spun. He's the one! He's the one who's making us spin! All the other mes turned to look at the big me. And what do you know, the big me's eyes were plastered over with the eyes of nutrition. Teeheehee. The vulgar tittering reached a crescendo, the wheel speeding up along with it until it was spinning too fast to distinguish with the naked eye. *BAM.* A loud sound and the smell of charred meat wafting on the air, and then suddenly, *BOOM.* Every me was blown to smithereens, pulverized and scattered, and with that, all my consciousnesses went dark. A mist of blood sprayed in all directions, a rainbow in the blue sky.

A deafening roar, and my eyes snapped open. I found myself lying half-naked in the grass on the outskirts of the airport. My head was pounding. I spotted my muddy coat lying a little ways away. My pants were caked with mud, too, and my watch and wallet were gone. Mortified tears flowed down my cheeks and fell among the grass. I tried clenching and unclenching my fists.

My fingers were black as pitch. Which meant my face probably was as well, the tears leaving muddy streaks in their wake. I must look insane right now. Pathetic. Salt in the air. Am I near the ocean? I'm parched.

I pulled up a handful of grass and started wiping off my face, at which point I saw a man in white walking toward me from the direction of the airport buildings. I couldn't let anyone see me in such a wretched state. I picked up my coat and tried to brush the mud off, then threw it over my shoulders and buttoned it up, acting for all the world like I was just out there for a casual stroll. The white-clad man was heading straight for me. Was he going to chew me out?

"Hello."

"Hello."

"Out for a stroll?" he asked with a smile. Seemed like he wasn't going to chew me out after all. I matched my tone to his.

"Yes indeed. The weather was so nice, I just didn't want to stop, and I ended up all the way out here."

"That's all very well, then. Though, that is..."

The man pointed at a white building over yonder that looked like a curving folded screen, and choking up, he continued, "Are you staying at the Grand Rich Hotel?"

"I am indeed. I make a habit of staying there every year around this time."

"Must be nice."

"Well, you know, now that you mention it, I find I'm a bit tired. Must've overdone it on the walk. If you'll excuse me," I said. "Excuse me," and, turning on my heel, I started off toward the Grand Rich Hotel. Kahaha. I really pulled one over on him. I wonder if he really was an airport employee or what. After two or three steps I turned to look back, and in that instant a flash of light. White light flooded my eyes, and I toppled back into the grass with a thud. Rain on the soles of my shoes. Graupel. Bellowing.

"You fucker, you dumb asshole, you're a fucking bum, aren't you? You're a thief, aren't you? Naked, feh, naked and covered in mud, what kind of bullshit are you trying to spout, you dumb fuck. A bum like you could never be a guest at the Grand Rich Hotel. I can't even get a room in a place like that!" My head ached. Dull blows in between the bursts of bellowing, so I curled up in the fetal position, protecting the back of my head with both hands. "What were you planning on stealing, huh? You fucking fuck. The fertilizer that disappeared from the warehouse, that was you too, wasn't it, you fuck. I'll kill you, I swear!" A sharp pain in my forehead & a blinding light.

And don't come back. You hear me? Dumb fuck. After shoving me out of the bed of the truck, the guy got back into the driver's seat and drove off with a booming report. When I finally managed to get up and look around, a shallow stream was running to my left, woods dead ahead. There was a massive torii standing at the entrance to the trees. The water followed the edge of the wood in a wide arc, sparkling in the light.

I was violently thirsty. I knelt on the bank of the stream and thrust my face into the water. It was bracing. The water. Its taste. My expectations were brutally betrayed. Sliminess, spreading through my mouth. The taste of shit. I spewed the water back out. And the next instant, I felt a bizarre sense of movement on my face, suction, and stepping back in consternation, I looked at the stream. The surface of the water, painted red and blue and yellow, was alive with rippling motion. A school of carp were going wild. It was more like a river of carp with some water mixed in than the other way around. I've never seen so many carp in all my life. Still parched.

What do you call that thing? A spout? No, that's just the top part. C'mon, you see them all the time at shrines, water coming out of a dragon's mouth, stone cistern underneath. Dammit, what's it called. With the ladle. A stoup? I can't remember, but whatever, there oughta be one of those around. I walked across the gravel and under the torii into the shrine grounds, but no dice. I guess the whole forest was holy ground, cedar trees lining the wide, magnificent ceremonial path on either side. The place was dotted with torii, moss-covered stone walls, sacred ropes cordoning off impressive rocks, but no water fountains shaped like dragons. Maybe there'll be one if I go all the way to the inner sanctum? Walking on gravel makes me feel unsteady, wobbly, like I'm about to lose my balance, but there's also that sense of security that comes from really tramping it down. Walking like that awakens a feeling of piety. But there's no time for that, I'm parched. Here and there, youths bearing short swords and bronze mirrors are prostrating themselves.

At the end of the path, a giant stone wall and a dry moat. Stone steps on the far side. The main hall must be at the top of those steps. I crossed the stone bridge over the moat, deer and cranes wriggling on the bottom below me. But I'd been duped. There's not a god damn thing here. There's nothing at all. All that buildup made it seem like there had to be a truly majestic hall of worship at the end, but at the top of the steps there's no shrine or anything, just an empty plot of land, a vague vacant lot, weeds growing around the border like a hedge, with empty bento boxes, a propane stove, food scraps littered all around, and not a drop of water to be seen. Now I'm pissed. Really pissed. It's always like this. There's never anything at the end of the road. If this is the deal, don't make it seem like there's a shrine, god dammit, and a big one at that. Staggering around the empty plot of land half in a rage, I. am. fucking. parched! but then again half consumed with pathetic misery because my throat is killing me like it's all coated with dust and cockleburs, I end up over on the opposite side from where I came up the stone steps, and there's a glittering band of light. A river. A giant Ferris wheel beside it. The light glinting off the windshields of the cars racing along the road atop the embankment, the sound of their horns, the scent of exhaust, they reach all the way up here to this bogus shrine. There's water over there. There are words. I can harp on this bogus shrine all I want, but it won't do any good. Time to go. Here I go. Back to the human realm. Peering over the edge, the slanted stone retaining wall continues down about thirty feet. Beyond that, a slope of cedars. I gingerly descended the stone, then headed down the tree-studded hillside. I could see the Ferris wheel between the branches the whole time.

I could see the Ferris wheel. From far off it looked truly impressive, but close up it was a tiny, wretched thing. The plastic windows were clouded with white scratches, and time had not been kind to the childish fairy-tale paint job—the Ferris wheel equivalent of an old geezer doddering around in a fairy costume. Truly the lamest Ferris wheel I've ever seen in my life. Truly, genuinely wretched. A parched beast.

"Did you say something?" asked Satoe. Flustered, I tried to play it off. "Nope, I didn't say anything." The roof of the suburban department store was deserted. Go-karts and a Ferris wheel maybe fifteen feet across. Closed-up food stalls. A pet shop with no animals in sight. The children who used to play there now worn out and middle aged. A dead rooftop amusement park. Maybe the games and rides used to have more of a fairy-tale aura, but now the paint was peeling and they just looked desolate. Faded plastic benches dotted the place. They were a little low for eating, though, I guess, because Satoe, in her white blouse, red pleated skirt, and black socks, was bent forward uncomfortably over her yakisoba, bringing her face down to the plate and holding back her drooping hair with her left hand.

"Really? It sounded like you just said something about being parched."

"Well, yeah, I am thirsty, it's true."

"Oh, then here." Satoe held out a plastic bottle. I took it with a nod, and drank. It was delicious. "Mmm, this tea's delicious, huh," I said, but Satoe didn't answer. She just asked, "What time is it? Still too early?"

"I think they should be opening the doors soon."

"You were so antsy to get here, you hustled us out of the house way too early. And this is what we get. I wish you'd just let me take my time."

"But, it's better than being late, isn't it?"

"It's not a concert or a play or something. It's just an art opening, it's fine to get there a little late. But you just kept telling me to hurry up, and now here we are," said Satoe, half smiling. Yeah, you're right. Let's go, I said to appease my wife, and stood up. We started ambling towards the gallery where Yoshihara's exhibition was being held.

The entrance to the stairwell was like a black pit. A tear in the fabric of space. The wind carried a musty odor. Beneath my feet, the ground felt terribly unsteady. But to all outward appearances, I was walking just fine. Outwardly I appeared to be walking normally. An airplane rent the sky once more. Looking over my shoulder before I entered the pit—nothing but blue sky. Putrefying and ripped to shreds.

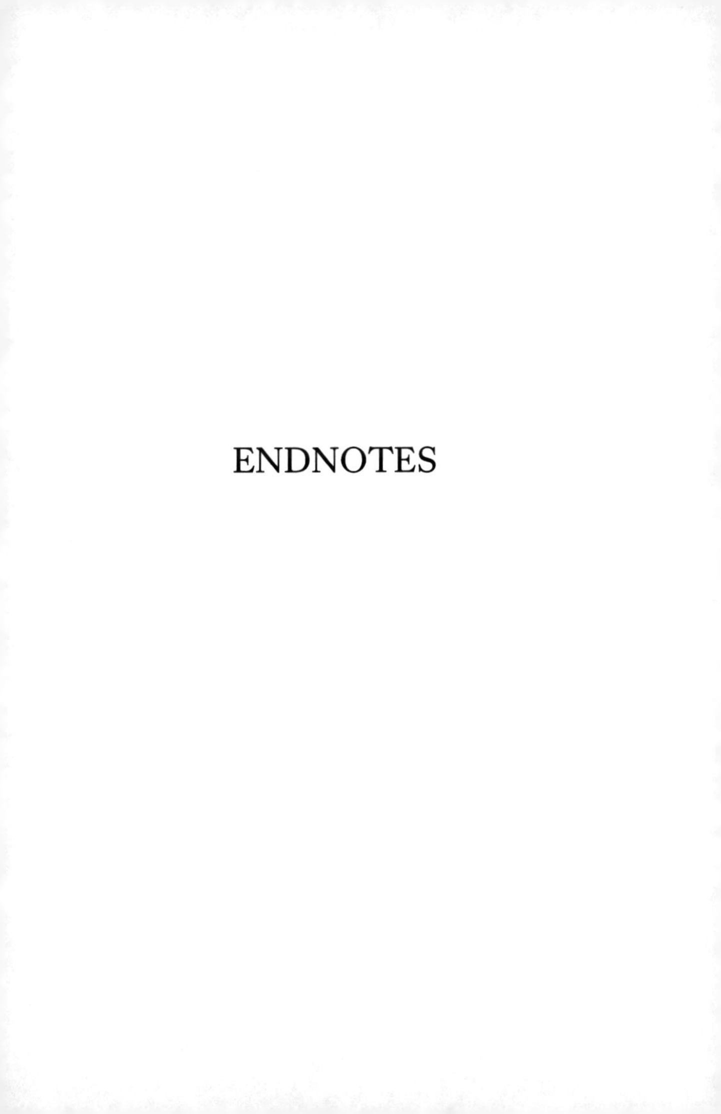

ENDNOTES

Daikokutens and Kisshotennyōs – Daikokuten is one of the Seven Gods of Good Fortune, with syncretic roots in Indian Buddhism and Japanese tradition, and presides over commerce and fertility (both sexual and agricultural), among other things. He is usually depicted carrying a mallet and sack of treasures, and standing or sitting atop two bales of rice. Kisshotennyō, likewise adapted from Hinduism via Buddhism, is a goddess of happiness, fertility, and beauty. Often conflated with the goddess Benzaiten, she is also sometimes included as one of the Seven Gods of Good Fortune in her own right. She is typically depicted holding a wish-granting jewel.

Shin·ichi no Hashi – Insofar as it takes place anywhere but the narrator's mind, *Rip It Up* seems to be set in a loose version of Tokyo. "Taking a taxi from the ANA Hotel towards Shin·Ichi no

Hashi" suggests central Tokyo, as does the subsequent reference to the department store Mitsukoshi, though one wouldn't actually pass it on the route described. Namikichō and Nigiwaichō are the only neighborhoods specifically mentioned in the book, the former common enough that there are two of them in Tokyo alone, while the latter exists only in Osaka, Nagoya, and Nagasaki as far as I know. This is not the only geographical inaccuracy or impossibility that the book asks us to accept, however, so let's just go with it.

Fukusuke dolls go back to the Edo period (1603-1868), and are meant to bring good fortune. They typically take the form of a man with a cartoonishly large head seated formally in the traditional dress of the period, and wearing the stereotypical *chonmage* hairstyle (shaved on top, with the gathered hair brought forward across the crown of the head) which will be familiar to anyone who's ever watched a samurai movie.

The singer and actress ***Misora Hibari*** (1937-1989) was a ubiquitous, not to say dominant, cultural presence in Japan in the mid-20th century. After making her debut at the age of nine, she was immediately hailed as a singing prodigy, and went on to release dozens of albums and hundreds of singles, many of which have sold millions of copies. She also appeared in well over a hundred movies, and is one of the most famous and recognizable Japanese celebrities of all time.

Setsubun marks the day before the first day of spring by the old Japanese calendar, now celebrated around February 3rd. Among the many rituals associated with the holiday, the most important and most salient here is the practice of *mamemaki* (bean-scattering), in which the home is purified by pelting someone dressed as an *oni* (a traditional ogre or demon) with soybeans. The women at the Setsubun monster party are dressed in all manner of demonic guises, including *rakshasa*, flesh-eating demons originating in Hindu mythology who also figure prominently in Buddhism, and Gozu and Mezu, the ox- and horse-headed guardians of Hell.

Marriage interviews – The practice of *omiai*,

in which prospective marriage partners meet to assess one another's suitability (sometimes with their families and/or a go-between in attendance), originated in the 16th century as a means for the warrior class to cement alliances. While lineage and social standing were formerly prime considerations, these have become less important in contemporary *omiai*. The practice has dropped off sharply in recent years, with somewhere around 6% of marriages still arranged this way (though the number was somewhat higher when this book was written in the late 1990s).

Lake Onokoro doesn't exist, but Onokoro (or Onogoro) is the legendary name of the first island created by the gods Izanagi and Izanami in the Japanese creation myth.

Yoshida Yoshizō is likewise not a real person, but seems to be a veiled reference to the author's own stage name, Machida Machizō. The characters with which this name is written could be read in other ways, and Machida consciously refuses to provide guidance on names, preferring to leave the choice up to the reader's imagination, but since it's my imagination doing the choosing here, this is what you get.

Isshin Tasuke is a well-known fictional character who embodies the virtues of an Edokko, or "true son of Edo." He appeared originally in kabuki plays and other Edo-period works, and later in film, television, manga etc.

Natsume Sōseki (1867-1916), the author of novels such as *Kokoro* and *Botchan*, is one of the foundational writers of modern Japan. *I Am A Cat*, a social satire told from the perspective of a pompous cat, was originally serialized in the literary journal *Hototogisu* in 1906-7.

Ame no Uzume no Mikoto – In a famous episode from the early myth-histories of Japan, the sun goddess Amaterasu (from whom the imperial house of Japan claims direct descent) shut herself up in a cave, thereby depriving the world of light. The goddess Ame no Uzume no Mikoto cleverly drew her out again by baring her breasts and performing a lascivious dance to the great amusement of the assembled gods.

Urashima Tarō is a universally known folk character in Japan, often compared to Rip Van Winkle. Many different variations of his tale exist, but in the most common version, Tarō rescues a turtle and in return is invited to enjoy the hospitality of the Dragon King's undersea palace. Returning to the surface after a few days (or years), he discovers that 100 (or 700) years have passed.

Obon, which takes place in mid-to-late summer depending on the region, is one of the most important Japanese holidays. It is a Buddhist celebration venerating the spirits of dead ancestors, but is perhaps best known outside Japan for its lively festivals and the accompanying group dance known as "Bon odori."

Emperor Sutoku (1119-1164) was the 75th emperor of Japan according to the official reckoning, and is known among other things for becoming one of the most infamous vengeful spirits of Japan after his death. The poem quoted here is number 77 from the *Ogura Hyakunin Isshu* (One Hundred Poets, One Poem Each) compiled by the great poet and scholar Fujiwara Teika in the early 13th century.

Marunouchi Building – The original Marunouchi building (so named because it stood in the Marunouchi neighborhood of Tokyo) was a famous landmark, and was one of the first buildings in Japan to combine offices with retail and restaurants. It was demolished in 1999 (right around the time *Rip It Up* was written) to make way for a new 37-story skyscraper, which was completed in 2002. Nicknamed the "Marubiru" in Japanese, it is not to be confused (or is it?) with the circular skyscraper in Osaka which bears the same nickname ("maru" means 'round' or 'circle').

"Toshishun" is a story by the Taishō-era author Akutagawa Ryūnosuke, a master of the strange and fantastic who is often referred to as the "father of the Japanese short story." It is loosely based on an ancient Chinese tale, and concerns a young man who repeatedly squanders his wealth. Along the way he notices that while people fawn over him when he's rich, they treat him with contempt when he's poor.

Both the menacing New Year's card the narrator finds and the passages from the *Diamond Sutra* are written in ***kanbun***, a form of Classical Chinese that was used in Japan from around the 8th century through the 20th. Its prestige made it the official language of the early court, and for centuries it remained the medium for intellectual discourse in much the same way Latin did in Europe. At this point it is difficult even for Japanese people to read without special training, and the New Year's card is of course rendered even more difficult by the fact that it makes very little sense.

General Sicklegrass – This name (Kamakusa no Shōshō in Japanese), is probably an oblique reference to the character Fukakusa no Shōshō, who appears in tales and literature as the often cruel lover of the famous 9th-century poet and legendary beauty Ono no Komachi.

The Thirty-Six Stratagems is an ancient Chinese strategic manual, which focuses on deception and subterfuge as means to achieve victory.

It has been attributed variously to Sun Tzu and others, but while its origins are unclear, it is well over a thousand years old at the very least.

Yukata – A light unlined cotton kimono, original worn to the bathhouse but now common at summer festivals and more broadly.

Torii – A ceremonial gate which marks the entrance to a Shinto shrine or sacred space. Usually but not always made of wood and painted red.

Kou Machida is a punk singer, actor, and author, who turned to poetry and fiction after releasing one of the seminal Japanese punk albums with his band INU, 1981's *Meshi kuuna!* (Fuck Eating!). He has won the Akutagawa and Tanizaki prizes among many others, and his 2005 novel *Kokuhaku* (Confession) was named one of the three best books of the last thirty years by the *Asahi Newspaper*.

Daniel Joseph is a translator, editor, and musician who spent his salad days shouting in dank basements before getting a master's degree in medieval Japanese literature. Recent translation projects include contributions to *Terminal Boredom* (Verso, 2021), a collection of stories by science fiction pioneer Izumi Suzuki; and the memoir *Try Saying You're Alive!* (Blank Forms, 2021) by outsider folk maniac Kazuki Tomokawa.